SAM'S DIARY

BoB —

Thanks for your
support!

Hélie

Sam's Diary

H. L. Bailey

iUniverse, Inc.
New York Lincoln Shanghai

Sam's Diary

iUniverse, Inc.

For information address:
iUniverse, Inc.
2021 Pine Lake Road, Suite 100
Lincoln, NE 68512
www.iuniverse.com

ISBN: 0-595-31763-4

Printed in the United States of America

For Ruth, Abby and Maggie
with love and thanks

Grateful acknowledgment is made to:

Betty Smith, R.N., Laurie and Lynn Duncan, and Ruth Wise for their invaluable support and assistance, and to my three children who were my inspiration.

PROLOGUE

❁

ℭ

My dearest daughter:

I did it, I finally got up enough courage to do it. I waited a long time, but I did it. At times I had my doubts that I would ever do it, but I did it. I can just hear you, Sam, "Mom, you are so boring. Stop talking in circles and tell me what the hell you mean by 'I did it'". Fair enough. I have come to the end of my "I did its" anyway and I cannot postpone the moment any longer. Here I go: Sam, I read your diaries, which you kept all through high school. There, it's out, all in the open now, and I feel a little relieved after making this confession.

When I was reading your diaries, I could actually visualize you sitting in your room, probably on your bed, surrounded by a mess, writing down your thoughts, ideas, hopes, dreams and complaints, and I caught myself talking to you. This gave me the idea to copy parts of your diaries, give my comments on these excerpts in writing and present the whole thing to Dad one of these days, probably on his birthday or on one of our wedding anniversaries.

It is not feasible to give my views on every entry you made. Even if I were so inclined, I would not be able to do it for the simple reason that many pages dealt with school acquaintances or events I cannot identify with. Consequently, I have carefully selected only those pages in which you described incidents relating to you, your family, and some of your friends I knew.

Sam, honey, thank you for keeping diaries, for not destroying them and for trusting me, your mother, out of all people, to read them.

All my love.

Always, mom

CHAPTER 1

❀

(September)

I finally cleaned up my room. As far as I was concerned, it was not really as messy as it could be or has often been. I really don't care what it looks like, but evidently, Mom did. She said that if it was not straightened up by early afternoon, I could not go to Steve's party tonight.

Big deal. I told her that I am not very crazy about Steve anyway and that I wouldn't mind missing his party, and that way, I could leave my room just the way it is until I am invited to a better event, but she did not go for that suggestion at all. As a matter of fact, she totally ignored what I said. She just gave me three plastic bags and told me to get after it. When I started arguing (I really am very good at that), she gave me a short version of her "be responsible" speech. Since I have heard it many, many times before, I did not listen all that well, but I did catch the part that has something to do with not being able to use the phone for a while, and that did it. I love talking on the phone, so I reluctantly went upstairs and got started.

Cleaning up my room took forever. At least two hours. It does look pretty good, though. I found a lot of things I thought I had lost: CD.'s, a pair of jeans, an old letter from Grandma with a ten dollar bill in it (I bet I forgot to write her a "Thank You" note), my eighth-grade school picture (my worst picture ever), a diary, and gym shorts I thought I had lost. I put the shorts in the bottom of one of the bags, because I remember how pissed Mom was when I couldn't find them or the other pair the first week of school and she had to write a check for another pair.

I had completely forgotten about this diary. Think I got it last Christmas and, until now, I have never written one word in it.

I asked Mom what you write in a diary and she said, "whatever you want to or anything you don't feel you can talk about, not even with me." Well, in that case, I should not have any trouble finding things to write about.

Anyway. My name is Samantha Evers, but everyone calls me "Sam." I am going to be fifteen next month and I am a freshman in high school in Austin. School sucks majorly most of the time, but I kinda like it anyway. So far, I am doing pretty well in all my subjects, especially Honors English, which is my favorite class.

I have one brother, Dean, who is sixteen and a sophomore. He is quiet and pretty good looking for a brother and he is very smart. He loves Country and Western music and all he wears are jeans and boots. Mom always says that he is so easy to buy clothes for. He has never even had a date yet, and I sure don't understand that. The day I am turning sixteen, boys, watch out, here I come and I am going to start dating, dating and dating. Dean does not seem all that interested in girls. He likes to be by himself and he doesn't participate in many school activities, except track. He is tall and kinda dark, like Dad. I am short and have dark blond hair, which I would love to color several shades lighter, but Mom told me that would have to take place over her dead body.

Dad's name is Brian and he is an architect. He designed the house we live in and it is beautiful. He doesn't talk very much, but he is funny and I love him. Sometimes, Mom gets a little pissed when Dad does not say much or doesn't what she calls "communicate." "Communicate" is one of her favorite words and she uses it in her speeches whenever she lectures me or Dean, mostly me. I think that Mom and Dad are happily married. They don't fight or argue very much and they laugh a lot. We also do a lot of things together. "Doing things together as a family" is something else that Mom feels she has to mention frequently.

Mom's name is Helen and she doesn't do anything, except teach aerobics a few times a week, and she is very much into sports. Dad is kinda good looking, but Mom is plain and not very pretty. I love her, but sometimes, no very often, she drives me absolutely up the wall.

I have quite a few friends, but my closest friend is Pam. We have known each other since first grade. Until I met her, everyone called us "Samantha" and "Pamela", but when we got to be friends, it was just sorta changed to "Sam" and "Pam". Pam is very pretty and she makes straight A's without having to study much. She is quiet most of the time and she never gets excited about anything, like I do. I love to get all worked up over things. Pam has two younger sisters, Kimberley and Joyce and they live with their mother, who is divorced.

Her mom's name is Emma and she and Mom are real good friends and they teach that aerobics crap together. Pam's mom does a lot of yelling at her kids, but they are all crazy about her. She also knows every cuss word on earth, but she tries not to use bad language when we're around.

Pam only sees her dad a few times a year. Her mom does not want to see him ever again. Pam said that one time her mom was talking to her grandma on the phone and she heard her say that she didn't care if she ever saw that S.O.B. again, as long as the rich mother-fucker kept sending her alimony checks on time. I asked Pam what her grandma thought of all that bad language, and Pam said that it was a purely genetic thing. One time, mom accidentally said "shit" in front of Grandma, and Grandma quickly crossed herself, although she is not Catholic.

Pam's mother and Mom have been teaching that boring aerobics for years. Last month, just before school started, Pam's dad took her and her sisters to Disneyland, and Emma came over quite a lot. One time, when Dean and I were eating dinner, Mom and Emma were talking in the other room. They were saying that, sometimes, they were just getting real tired of doing the same thing over and over, week after week, and Pam's mom said that she either had to give up smoking or aerobics, because "all that shitty running in place crap is killing me." and "sometimes I don't give a fuck if those fat farts don't ever lose an ounce." Dean and I overheard every word and we laughed.

Cannot think of anything else to write about. This diary is not bad at all, and I may just start writing in it regularly. Am going to take a shower and ask Mom to wash the jeans I found earlier, so that I can wear them to Steve's party tonight. Hope she doesn't say something stupid like, "Sam, you are going to a party tonight. Don't you think it would be nice if you wore a skirt or a dress for the occasion?" Mom, I only own two dresses and I hate them both, and no, thank you very much, I do not want to wear a skirt. I want to wear my jeans. That was not quite fair of me. Mom doesn't ever criticize what I wear. Think it has to do with the fact that she doesn't like dresses either and wears shorts or jeans most of the time.

(Later)

I just talked to Pam on the phone and we both decided that we feel sorry for Steve and we're never going to make fun of him again, and Pam is never going to imitate him again, which is too bad, because she does it so well.

Steve had invited about twenty-five kids, but only fourteen showed up and most of them were girls. That was the first party he had ever given, and Pam and I thought that was pretty obvious. We really did not do anything. Just sat around, played table tennis, ate popcorn, drank punch, and listened to the worst music we had ever heard. We could not figure out what it was, but Macie knew all about it. Macie lives with her grandmother and, evidently, her grandmother listens to all sorts of old fart music and that's exactly what we were subjected to.

Think everybody was pretty happy when it was time to be picked up. I know Pam and I were. We really feel sorry for Steve. He and his family belong to some kind of church that does not believe in celebrations of any kind, not even Christmas. I wonder what they do for fun? The only thing they observe is birthdays, but no presents, thank you very much. Since this was Steve's first party, it was probably also the first time he received gifts. What a bummer! I had bought him a gift certificate for a CD. or whatever, and when his mother, who stayed in the room with us the entire evening, saw the certificate, she said, "Oh Stevie, isn't that thoughtful of Samantha? Now you can buy that new Precious Souls album." Dave Miller asked her who Precious Souls was and she acted as if we should all know that they were a very inspiring and popular Christian group. Dave was going to give Steve a poster of a girl in a wet bathing suit, sipping a beer, but he didn't, which is too bad, because it would have been very interesting to find out what Steve's mother would have said, although I can guess.

Steve has at least six brothers and sisters and they all look alike. They live in a big house, but it is not cozy at all. There are no books around, no pictures on the wall, except some Jesuses, no knick-knacks, like we have everywhere in the house and which Mom hates to dust but keeps on buying anyway.

Pam and I are really going to be nicer to Steve from now on. We think.

❈   ❈   ❈

I remember Steve very well. In your sophomore year, you and he were in the same biology class, which was taught by Woods, or whatever his name was. He was not a very kind or compassionate man, and, according to what you told us, he made Steve the butt of his sarcasm. Steve never said a word, until one day when he had obviously had enough. He told Woods very politely to "screw off." Steve had been relatively friendless until that moment, but that timid, little, "screw" earned him some respect and he even made some friends, which he needed so badly. When Dad and I went to a PTA meeting, Dad had the misfortune to meet this teacher and he said that he could not stand him. That was quite a statement coming from Dad, who was so kind and who always had a good word to say about everyone he met.

Dad knew Steve's father, who worked for a mortgage company. He said he was a real pleasant guy, but a little "hen-pecked." I told Dad to keep up with the times—men were no longer "hen-pecked", but "pussy-whipped."

When Dad and I picked you and Pam up after the party and when you were discussing the evening and were wondering what they did for fun, Dad whispered to me, "I don't know what all those kids do for fun, but I know what the parents do for entertainment. They screw a lot." Shame on you, Brian.

I have seen Steve only once in the past three years, and that was about six months ago or so. He is going to college and wants to be a teacher. He is dating a nice looking girl and they are living together. Sam, you know that I am not a prude, but I never believed in young, unmarried people sharing an apartment and their bodies and whatever else it is they share. Truthfully, I don't know why I feel so strongly about that. Dad and I lived together for a short while before we got married, so why can't I accept that in other people? Pretty hypocritical on my part. Anyway, when Steve so proudly volunteered the information that he was living with this nice looking young lady, who was holding his hand so proudly and sweetly, I set all my reservations aside and told him how happy I was for the both of them, and I meant every word of it. I also asked him if he remembered his birthday party and if he had bought that inspiring CD. with it. He said, "Oh no, Mrs. Evers. Of course not. Don't quite remember what I spent it on, but I know for a fact that it was something entirely different." Steve has changed so much and I was somewhat surprised and slightly disappointed that he didn't say, "Shit no, Helen. Are you kidding?"

You are right, Sam. Emma is a strikingly beautiful woman. She is also one of the nicest persons one can hope to meet and she is my dearest friend. She has a wonderful sense of humor and she needed it, being a single parent, raising three daughters.

We all know that Emma's language was a little rough at times, but that was just part of her and it never bothered me or Dad. When I said "shit", it sounded just like that and nothing more. Emma had a soft and melodious voice and she could make any four-letter word sound like it should belong in a sonnet. The first time I met Emma was at a PTA meeting right after you and Pam started first grade. She was sitting next to me and she mumbled that the principal's speech was so "fucking boring" and it was. I asked Emma once how she managed to still sound like a lady when she was cussing and she said that it was a precious gift and, also, that you could say any expletive, just as long as you crossed your ankles in a ladylike fashion while uttering them. This made absolutely no sense. Emma often made no sense, but that's one of the many things I like so much about her.

Emma rarely mentioned her ex-husband and she adamantly refused to talk about the reasons for her divorce. However, she once mentioned that he was very charming and pretty experienced in bed (of course, Emma did not use that many words) but that, unfortunately, he willingly and proudly shared his talents with a lot of women. He was and still is a very successful lawyer in California. As far as Emma was concerned, the West coast was not far enough for him. She had Micronesia or Romania in mind. The only nice thing Emma ever said about him was that he was extremely generous and that she was happy she was not out in the job world.

Emma and I got a lot of satisfaction out of teaching several aerobics classes, but we gave it up in your junior year. The club where we had been working, changed hands and the new owner wanted some "new blood" in the place. Emma and I saw the writing on the wall and we quit before he asked us to leave. Emma was thrilled, because now she saw absolutely no reason at all to give up smoking.

Before I forget, Sam. What exactly did you mean when you referred to me as "plain"? Couldn't you have been a little less harsh and less honest, lie just a tad and call me at least "ordinary"?

Yes, Sam, you were right about Dad and me being happy together. We have our disagreements, but they don't last long. He is the salt of the earth, a kind, wonderful man with a great sense of humor and not only do I love him, I am still in love with him.

CHAPTER 2

❀

(October)

I had every good intention of writing in this diary every night, but I either forgot or, sometimes, when I thought about it, I was not in the mood. I have only written a few times and it all sounds so friggin' boring. It's almost time to go to bed, but I am going to spend a few minutes writing about today, which was one of the worst days of my life.

I took a math test, which was hard and I think I royally screwed up on two problems. I got an 82 back on a history test, which I thought I had aced. I did not stop talking in one of my other classes and now have detention tomorrow. I also lost my lunch money again.

I could not wait to get home and complain to Mom about this terrible day, but what does she do when I walk through the door? Does she give me sympathy? No. She gave me this bag from a department store and asks me to go to my room and try them on to see if they fit.

"Them" were bras and today was just not the day for me to bother with those stupid things. And why do I need to wear one anyway, when I am still absolutely and totally flat? Well, at least almost. Mom told me that I am now fifteen (thank you, mother, I was not aware of my age and I am so grateful that you pointed this out to me) and in high school and that I should start wearing one, especially in P.E., boobs or no boobs, and whether I like them or not.

Last year, when I was in eighth grade, we went through the same thing, but then I got away with it. Somehow, I don't think that is going to happen again this time, since Mom was pretty insistent and when she gets that way she can also get quite obnoxious.

Anyway, I tried them on and they look pretty stupid and, of course, they don't fit and how could they? I yelled at Mom that she had wasted her money, but she did not comment. Just asked me not to make such a production and to be sure to wear one to school every day. Then she lied to me and said that I would soon get used to them. Don't know how many girls in school wear one, but I know that Pam has for at least a year.

When Dad got home that evening, he gave me a hug and rubbed my back. I got mad and told him not to do that. Dad looked surprised and said that he didn't know what I was talking about and that he has given me a hug and a quick back scratch every night when he comes home from the office, for as long as he can remember. I thought that I had better explain this awkward situation to him and said, "I am sure that Mom called you at the office and told you that she bought some bras for me and you only scratched my back to see if I was wearing one."

That remark got Mom all started. She said, "Sam, honey, how did you guess? I called dad's office this afternoon and asked the receptionist to turn up the intercom full blast. Then I announced to the entire office that Sam Evers, age fifteen, would, by 3:15 this afternoon, be the proud owner of five brassieres in assorted colors." She was laughing and Dad had no idea what we were talking about. I wanted to say something, but she started to roll her eyes and I figured I had better shut up. Besides I wanted to go to my room and laugh about what Mom had said. She can be pretty funny at times.

Mom is not the right person to tell me to wear those damned things anyway. I know for a fact that she doesn't like them herself, because she told me one time that the persons who had invented the bra and pantyhose were "feeble minded". Also, I just remember that one time, on the way home from the movies, she was squirming in the front seat. Dad asked her what her problem was and she told him that she was just taking her "damned" bra off. Then she threw it on the back seat. It touched me and that grossed me out totally. Dad could not believe it either and he said, "Honey, you mean to tell me that you are doing this in the middle of traffic on Interstate 35?" and Mom, the smart-ass, said, "Well yes, Brian, Would you rather I had waited until we got to highway 290?" And this is the woman telling me what to wear.

Pam called a while ago and wanted to know what I was so mad about. She said that wearing one is no big deal and she didn't understand why I was so ticked off. Truthfully, I don't know either. Maybe it would be nice if I went downstairs and told Mom that I am slightly sorry about the way I acted, but maybe I won't. Since I cannot make up my mind, I am just leaving things the way they are.

❧   ❧   ❧

Sam, please allow me to correct you. I never referred to those inventors as "feeble minded". I distinctly remember stating that they should merely be burned at the cross.

Yes, you really had a temper, but you came by it honestly. Dad and Dean were so quiet and easy going, but you and I were pretty excitable and it was no problem at all for us to get worked up over all sorts of situations, which, in all fairness, did not even deserve any discussion, let alone a heated one.

Whenever you had one of your outbursts, you reminded me so much of myself at that age. Neither one of us achieved much mature behavior in the first two years of attending high school, but I believe you did better than I did. I think I was still a pretty sad case when I graduated, but you were most definitely not.

CHAPTER 3

❀

(November)

Another month has passed and, again, I did not write much, except about dull stuff that happened in school and other unimportant things.

Truthfully, I really don't have time to write right now, because I am supposed to practice the blasted clarinet. Had been begging Mom and Dad for ages to let me take lessons and they finally gave in and what a mistake that was.

Anyway, Mom found a music teacher. She's a real nice lady. When we met her the first time, she wanted to know if I was dedicated and disciplined enough to practice forty-five minutes every day, including the week ends, and I told her that I was. Mom put in her two cents worth and told the lady that a more dedicated nor a more disciplined teenager could not be found in this hemisphere. On the way home she wanted to know if that had sounded like "ass-kissing".

The excitement wore off after taking the very first lesson. It has been a few months now and I hate every minute of it. Mrs. Cain told me the other day that I may progress more rapidly if I took two lessons a week instead of one, and I almost freaked out. She said that she would call my parents, and I quickly told her that I would take care of it. Needless to say, I had no intention of discussing this with either Mom or Dad and, at the next lesson, I just told her that we were sticking to just one lesson a week and that this was a unanimous decision. Was not too proud of lying, but got over this guilt feeling by the time I got home.

Truthfully, I would not mind practicing if I could just forget about scales and all that crap and play what I want. Mom and Dad told me that everyone needs a break and that they thought it would be all right if I didn't touch the instrument on week ends. Dean, who, I believe, is getting sick and tired or listening to me, blessed both Mom and Dad for making this suggestion. Pam is taking piano lessons and she plays so well. The other day I took the clarinet over to her house and we played together. Sounded pretty damned good, even if I say so myself.

We had our first recital last night. Told Mrs. Cain a couple of weeks ago that I didn't think I was ready yet for such a grand event, but she insisted that all her students participate in this evening, which "means so much, especially to the parents." Don't think it meant much to Dad. He told mom last week that he might have a late meeting that evening and mom told him something like, "Brian, Sweetheart, I'll have your head on a platter if you don't show up." And show up he did. And so did Pam, which was great.

The recital went all right, but I felt like a two-year old having to play those two pieces that sounded very much like "Three Blind Mice". There were six piano players, two clarinets and three flutes and they all sounded a lot better than I did. Bet they practice more.

Playing in front of all those parents made me a little nervous and my hands got a little sweaty. We are having another recital in six weeks, but I fully intend not to participate in that one, due to the fact that I am going to convince Mom and Dad that I am wasting their money, which is a real shame, given the present economic situation. This sounds good, but I can see several loop holes and I had better work on my speech before approaching Mom and Dad.

Cannot think of anything else to write about. May as well play the clarinet for a while.

❧   ❧   ❧

Sam, honey, encouraging you to practice that damned instrument was an enormous challenge, because you could always come up with more excuses as to why you could not or did not have to practice. Some of them were pretty good and I agreed with you that practicing on the eve of a national holiday, the actual day itself, the day after and many other important dates would have been a disgrace and very, very, unpatriotic. Needless to say, there was no practice on the day you saw a dead squirrel in the road, or when the leaves started turning, or when the neighbor's dog started barking before 6:00 in the morning, or etc., etc., etc. Dean had the best suggestion. He thought you should never practice on the days the sun rose in the East.

You quit taking lessons before the second recital. I don't remember what reasons we gave Mrs. Cain, but I am convinced they were only half-truths.

I remember your first recital very well. I felt somewhat sorry for you, because you really did not play all that well yet and I don't think it was right of your teacher to ask you to be one of the participants. Dad was not very impressed either. He said that you sounded somewhat like I did in the last stages of giving birth to Dean. Not a very kind remark, but very true.

After you stopped the lessons, you started enjoying the clarinet a lot more and you became quite good at it and we always enjoyed listening to you and Pam playing together. Pam often brought out the best in you, and there was so much good in you.

Sam, your music lessons lasted considerably longer than your tap-dancing, your twirling, or gymnastics.

CHAPTER 4

❀

(December)

I am getting all excited about Christmas. Tomorrow, Dad is taking us to a lot to cut our own tree.

Mom and I love decorating the tree, but Dad and Dean don't participate much. Think they get tired of Mom and me discussing each little ornament for a long time before hanging it on the tree, but that's really the fun part. Also, I think Dean is embarrassed about seeing the decorations that he made when he was in grade school still being hung up every year. He asked mom how many more years she was going to do that and she said she would until they cancelled Christmas, and, since that was never going to happen, forever.

I am going to my first high school dance tonight and I am really looking forward to it. At first I was not going, since nobody had asked me and I lost interest. Then Bruce called. He is in my history class and he is pretty nice. He and his parents are picking me up at eight tonight, and then they'll drive me home after the party. I believe that his parents are chaperoning the evening. I would just die if Mom or Dad did that. A few weeks ago we received a note from our home room teacher, to find out if our parents were willing to help with the Christmas dance and do things like baking, chaperoning, or cleaning up. I was scared to death that Mom would decide that it might be nice to go to the party, so the note never found its way home.

Dad asked me if I was looking forward to my first high school dance and date, and I told him that I did not really consider this a date, since Bruce's parents were picking me up and that was not very exciting.

I wish I were old enough to drive. I am signed up to take Driver's Ed next month. Was dying to take it when I turned fifteen last October, but that didn't happen. Dad got pissed at me for doing something and he told me that I had to wait until January, or even later, if my attitude did not improve. With that prospect in mind, my attitude changed drastically overnight. Cannot even remember why Dad got so upset with me, but it must have been something major, because he hardly ever gets mad.

Cannot wait for my sixteenth birthday when I can drive all by myself. Dean said that he can wait easily, because when I have my license, he and I have to share the car he is driving now, which is Mom's and Dad's old car. Hope it all works out.

Anyway, as much as I hate to dress up, I am going to tonight. Asked mom if I should wear a dress or a skirt and blouse and she said that there was not much point in buying a dress and only wearing it once, and, for once, I had to agree with her. Pam's mom dropped Pam and me off at the mall and we spent hours going from shop to shop, and we almost forgot to buy something for the dance. We finally each bought a blouse and skirt and it looks pretty nice. I also had to buy a pair of shoes. Pam's mom was picking us up at five and, at that time, we had not even bought our outfits yet, so I bought the shoes in the biggest hurry and they don't feel all that good and I already know that they will never be worn again after tonight.

Am glad that Pam is also going tonight. She is so pretty and I know that a lot of boys like her, but she doesn't pay much attention to any of them. She said that there was no point in getting all worked up over a boy when she is not allowed to date until she turns sixteen. Think Emma and Mom got together on that one, since I also have to wait until that age. Even then, I am not allowed to go out with just anybody, and Mom said she would really like to know whom I am going out with. Isn't that ridiculous? I asked her one time, "You mean to tell me that, when a boy picks me up, I have to introduce him to you?" And Mom said, "Not only to me, but to Dad, Dean, your grandparents if they happen to be visiting, the Avon lady, the UPS delivery person, and to any living creature within a two-mile radius." Her speeches can be so very boring, but she thought she was funny. And then she added something like me being married one of these days, having children of my own, and, wouldn't I like to know whom they were running around with? Well, yes, if you put it that way.

Dad wants me to be ready a little early tonight, so that he can take some pictures. I told him that was all right, just as long as he didn't take any after Bruce gets here. Dad said that he would have to think about that a little. Sometimes, he and Mom treat me like I am still a baby. I made the mistake one time of telling them this, and they said that they were fully aware of this fact and that, if I just acted a little more mature, they would end their infantile behavior immediately. Sometimes I feel that I cannot win.

Here I am, fifteen years old, and I have never even had a period yet. Mom said not to worry about it. She also started late, not until she was eighteen or so, well, maybe she was sixteen. Anyway, she said that I was fortunate, since periods are a royal pain and an invention by the devil.

(Later)

Got back from the dance a while ago and it was all right. Bruce sure is a nice guy. He is a little shy, but he did tell me that I looked pretty and that made me feel kinda good. Dean told me the same thing, well, not in that many words. Think he said that I cleaned up real nice. Dean's grammar sucks. The band was all right, but not a whole lot of people danced. We just sat around in groups all evening and we talked and laughed a lot. Bruce and I danced a few times and he was as bad as I am. His parents watched us the entire evening and his dad even got on the dance floor and took our picture. Bruce did not seem to mind at all.

Pam and her date danced a lot. They also weren't very good, but Pam didn't care. She said that she came to dance and that's what she did. She was wondering why Dean wasn't there. She often talks about him and I think she likes him. Come to think of it, Dean does a lot of hanging around us when she comes over.

It's almost one o'clock and I had better get ready for bed. Cannot sleep very late tomorrow since I have a shit load of homework for Monday. Wonder when our school is going to have another dance?

❧   ❧   ❧

Sweetheart, you really did look pretty that evening and very grown up and, after you and Bruce left, Dad and I talked about time going so fast and that it didn't seem possible that both of our children were in high school.

Sam, how can you say that my speeches were boring? I thought that they were often very entertaining and fairly effective. I just asked Dad's opinion and he volunteered the information that some of them were unquestionably long and a little on the dull side. Thank you, my Sweet. I am so happy I asked you.

By the way, Sam. It was a five-mile radius, not a two-mile one.

CHAPTER 5

❀

(January)

I really wanted to write in my diary over the holidays, but I didn't. I only wrote twice, and I think that I must either be very boring or lead an uneventful life, because most of the things I wrote about were not very interesting.

I am finally taking Driver's Ed. Started about two weeks ago and it really is not very thrilling. The class work is not too great, especially having to look at fifty-year old, black and white movies about terrible accidents.

There are four of us in the car, including the instructor, and you only get to drive for twenty minutes and I think that my twenty minutes are shorter than the other's. The rest of the time you have to sit there and that's not a whole of fun. We cannot eat or drink in the car, we cannot listen to the radio, because that is too distracting, and we cannot even talk. When I get my license, I am going to eat, drink, listen to the radio and talk all at the same time when I am driving. I have to take the test on Friday. Pam said that it was easy. She took it a couple of months ago.

I am lousy at parallel parking and I need to practice that a little more between now and the day I have to take the test. Mom said that she would not be much help in that department. She said that she tried parallel parking once, very unsuccessfully, and that she is never going to try it again as long as she lives or only when it is an absolute necessity, and, so far, she has never been in a situation where it was an absolute must.

This afternoon Mom put two trash cans in the road in front of the driveway and told me to practice parking in between them. Sounded like a good idea. I hit one trash can, but not too badly, but I hit the other one big time and it got stuck under the car and we could not get it out. When Dean got home, he jacked up the car and got it out. It took him a while, since he was laughing so much. He said that there was nothing to parallel parking, or driving in reverse, which I am also not very good at. Mom said that was easy for him to say. According to her, all men are born with a special gene, which allows them to maneuver a car any way they want to while having their eyes closed.

I told Dad what happened and he smiled. Said that I reminded him of Mom right after they got married. They only had one car and, most of the time, she drove him back and forth to work. He said that she was usually running a little late in the evening and that didn't bother him all that much, but one night she was really late and he started worrying a little. Then he looked out of his office window and there she was, trying to park their pride and joy between two other vehicles. She evidently put the car in reverse and hit the car behind her. Then, all flustered, she put the car in first gear and did major damage to the station wagon in front of her. Dad and I were laughing when he told me all this. He asked me not to tell any of this to Mom. Had something to do with her having an inclination to lose her sense of humor when it comes to certain things, and he was convinced that recollection of this little mishap might be one of those times.

(Later)

I passed the test and now I have my learner's permit and I have not stopped bugging Mom to go out and drive around. I must say that she has been pretty good about it. However, I hate for her to sit next to me. She wants to know if I saw the car in front of me, asks me not to get too close to a truck in front of me, because its brake lights might not be working, tells me to stop flirting with the guy sitting in a car in the lane next to us, although even she admitted that he was gorgeous, and said that she could explain why all the cars behind us were honking impatiently. Said she was sure they wanted me to take advantage of this green light before it turned a different color.

I am taking Dad out for a drive tonight. Bet he won't say anything.

Anyway, driving is great and I cannot wait to get my real license on my next birthday. Pam cannot wait either to get hers. As soon as we both have our license, we want to drive to Houston, go to AstroWorld, and do some shopping in the Galleria. I asked mom what she thought about that idea and she more or less indicated that this would have to happen over her dead body. Pam said that sounded very nice, considering what her mom told her when she made that suggestion.

Cannot think of anything else to write about. Need to do some homework and have to read five more chapters in *For Whom The Bells Toll*. It's pretty good, but I wish we didn't have to take notes. That takes the fun out of reading. English is, by far, my favorite subject and I really like Mrs. Sellers. She is so cool and nice and makes the class so enjoyable. The only thing I hate is grammar and sentence structure and all that punctuation crap. The other day we had to write a short story. After I got through typing it, I asked Mom to read it. She thought that it was very good and asked me who had written it. When I told her that it was none other than her daughter, she seemed so pleased and proud.

❀   ❀   ❀

Sam, how very audacious of Dad to tell you that story about my little driving incident in front of his office. And did he really call it a "little mishap"? He sure didn't refer to it as such when it happened and he acted like it was a major accident that would, more than likely, be printed on the front page of our local newspaper the next morning.

Did I really make all those banal comments when you were driving? I don't think so. How could I have, when I was engrossed in fervent prayer, begging God to get us home safely.

Yes, Dad often took you for a drive in the evening. One evening, after you both got home, he said that you were improving. Then he added that he had made a mistake in designing our house. Said that he should have made the garage opening several feet wider, and, that way, I would still have a rear view mirror.

Yes, your short stories were very good. We kept them all. Pam came over the other day when I happened to be going through them and she took a lot of them home to read. She is wonderful.

CHAPTER 6

❀

(February)

School is really going well and I am doing great in all my classes. However, I wish that I had never enrolled in this home economics class, which sucks greatly.

Fortunately, it is only for one semester. The teacher is a real dud and an old maid, at least fifty, and she sounds as if her class is the most important in the whole school and she acts as if we have no chance of ever succeeding in life, unless we successfully complete her course. She even gives us homework. Homework in sewing? Give me a break, please. I took that class for an easy A, lady. Pam cannot understand why I signed up for it either. There are even some boys in that class.

The first half of the semester we are sewing and the second half is going to be devoted to cooking. I asked Mom which was going to be the better of the two and she said that, as far as she was concerned, it was a toss-up between two activities she disliked intensely. She also wished that I had never taken that class and was afraid that it was going to be a long semester with a lot of parental help.

Our project for the next few weeks is to select a pattern and make something. Mom told me to choose anything rectangular or square, just in case she has to help me. Just in case she has to help me? I was going to ask her to make the whole thing for me, whatever it is.

Mom said that she took home economics in school and that it was her least favorite subject. She also took it for an easy A, but ended up with a C. A C in home ec, Mom? Anyway, she started on a lot of items, but only finished one. I asked her what she had handed in and she said that she would tell me only if I promised not to laugh. I promised. It was a little pillow case and I laughed anyway.

A couple of years ago, when I was in junior high and still wore dresses occasionally, Mom thought that it would be a nice idea if she made one for me because, after all, "how difficult can it be?" She asked me to choose a pattern and I also picked out the material and she started on it the same day, but it took her almost a whole year to finish it, so I guess that it was pretty difficult after all. When I tried it on, it didn't fit anymore and I didn't like it at all, and neither did Mom.

That night, when Dad got home, she asked him to put the sewing machine in the attic. Dad said that the attic was not a very handy place for it, since she wouldn't be able to get to it easily and she told him that was exactly the point, since she had no intention of ever using it again. Sometimes I really amaze myself. That conversation took place years ago and I remember it like it was yesterday. Dad told me one time that I had a fantastic memory when it came to remembering conversations, but he wished that I could not always repeat everything verbatim, especially not those conversations I was not supposed to listen to in the first place. Come on, Dad, those happen to be the best.

Dean got the sewing machine out of the attic after school today. Mom was going to explain to me how it worked, but she could not find the instructions and she could not thread the needle without it, but she kept on trying. I could tell by all her "damns" that she was getting frustrated, but she stuck with it. She finally did something and thought it was all set up properly. When I tried it, everything got all tangled up and we could not even get the material out from under the needle. Think she felt like screaming, but she didn't. Just took a pair of scissors and cut the material loose and said, "There now, wasn't that easy"?

I haven't told Mom yet, that when we start cooking, we have to keep track of all our meals for a whole week, because it would freak her out. We had to do that in junior high one time. All the meals had to contain items from the different food groups and it drove her up the wall. She said that she had never enjoyed cooking before, but liked it even less now. Then, when she went to a PTA meeting, the teacher told her that she was using entirely too much starch and fat. Mom was laughing when she got home and told Dad that she did not understand how this lady, who outweighed her by at least a hundred pounds, could feel comfortable lecturing her about starches and fats.

I had better stop writing now and get some shit done. Am glad it is Friday tomorrow. Pam and I and some of our friends want to go to the movies and then have some pizza. Just hate it that none of us have our driver's license yet and it is the pits to ask one of our parents. Maybe Dean will take us. Don't think he'll mind.

Mom just yelled upstairs and asked me to set the table. Since this little activity takes less than thirty seconds and since Mom is already downstairs, I don't understand why she cannot do it. Think I had better do it, though.

❧   ❧   ❧

Sam, you are so right. Home economics was an extremely sucky class. Do you know that we still have those two little place mats you made? I don't want to hurt your feelings, nor do I want to sound facetious, but I honestly believe that they were not as pretty as my little pillow case.

One week of fixing meals which contained all the right ingredients was enough to drive anyone insane, especially someone like me, who preferred to spend as little time as possible in the kitchen. Didn't I do well the first two days, though? After that I decided that there were more important things to concentrate on and we cheated badly on the assignment. Evidently, since the teacher criticized my menus, I didn't even do all that well preparing them on paper.

I want to say something in my own defense concerning my cooking. To be honest, the Evers family was not a delight to cook for. You were happiest with hamburgers, spaghetti, Mexican food, chicken or a salad, and, after preparing those meals for so many years, I got pretty good at them. Once in a while, I got the cookbook out and tried something different, but my efforts were not all that much appreciated. Dean mentioned one time that he was sure that the little urchins in Ethiopia would give their eyetooth for a meal like that but that, personally, he would be happier with a burger. Dad refused seconds, which was highly unusual for him, and you said that it looked too pretty to eat and only took a few bites. Truthfully, this meal which had taken me so long to prepare, was really not all that tasty and it did not remotely resemble the picture in the cookbook.

CHAPTER 7

❀

(March)

I don't feel like writing at all, but anything is better than being downstairs with grandma, so I told her that I had some homework to do and I went upstairs, where I am not doing homework.

Mom and Dad are skiing in Colorado. Dad had to be there on business, and Mom flew with him and she visited some friends in another town. When Dad got through with the meetings, they met in Steamboat and that's where they're skiing for a few days.

They left last Wednesday and won't be home till sometime next Saturday. They have called us several times and are having a good time. Dad said that the place they're staying in is beautiful and he is thinking about taking us all there for Christmas. Dean and I cannot wait.

Dean and I wanted to stay home by ourselves, but Mom and Dad were not too crazy about that, even though we think we're definitely old enough, and so I was going to Pam's and Dean was either going to stay home or go to a friend's house. That sounded good to us.

Then, Grandma called and screwed up our plans royally. Grandma and Grandpa hadn't seen us in a long time, and when Mom made the huge, unfor-givable mistake of telling her that she and Dad were going out of town for a while, Grandma immediately said that they would fly over and stay with us. Mom admitted making a big mistake, but there wasn't much anyone could do about it. I heard her tell Grandma over and over that we were old enough to stay by ourselves most of that time and that it was an extremely sweet offer (sweet offer, my ass) but that it was not necessary. Grandma and Grandpa are Dad's parents.

Anyway, I did get to spend a few nights at Pam's before Grandma and Grandpa flew in from Washington. Grandpa is a sweetie, but Grandma is something else and she complains all the time and tells everybody what they can and cannot do, mostly cannot.

All Grandma does is watch soap operas, cook, clean and bitch. Dean and I got out of school early today and when we got home, she was sitting on the couch with a box of Kleenex. I got kinda scared, because I thought that something had happened to Mom or Dad. Dean asked if she was all right and she sniffled, "Yes, I guess so, but I would feel so much better if he had not left her in her hour of need." It took me and Dean a few seconds to figure out that she was talking about her soap characters. Mom never watches them. She thinks that real life is pretty exciting and sometimes contains too much drama and she's not at all interested in all that crap.

Earlier tonight, Dean and I watched a 30-minute program downstairs. Grandma never shut up and talked throughout the entire half-hour. Then she said that she could not understand how we could possibly be engrossed in watching something that had so little educational value. I started telling Grandma that this program was far more superior than any of her damned soaps, but Dean interrupted me and said that we should go upstairs and he'd help me with an assignment.

I am sitting at my desk and Dean is reading a book in my bed. He hasn't turned a page in quite a while, and I think he's almost asleep. I just took a close look at him. He is handsome.

I told Dean that I sure don't like the way Grandma talks about Mom. She really doesn't say anything bad about her, but it is the way she words her sentences. Dean said that she does a lot of "insinuating."

The first night Grandma fixed supper, she asked me to set the table, so I quickly put the place mats, paper napkins and plastic cups on the table. Grandma looked astonished and said, "Samantha (never "Sam" mind you, it's too "boyish"), where on earth does your mother (never "mom") keep the table cloth and where are the linen napkins located?" She always sounds so formal, it drives me crazy. I told her that this was what we always used, except for Thanksgiving, Christmas and special occasions, (I wanted to add that her visit was definitely not a special occasion) and she thought that Mom had very bad habits. Grandma mumbled under her breath, but loud enough for me to hear, that Mom had terribly lazy behavior patterns. Did I say that Grandma sounds formal? Make that friggin' formal.

The next day she and grandpa went shopping and they came home with a real table cloth and napkins. I wanted to tell her that she had wasted her money, because we do own several sets of them, but I didn't. She might have asked me where they were and I have no idea. Probably somewhere up on a shelf in a closet, waiting to be ironed one of these days. Anyway, we sat down for dinner and Grandma told Dean and me to be careful and not get anything dirty. I told grandma that we were not three-year-olds and Dean kicked me under the table. I pretended that the kick was one of encouragement, so I added some other remarks, just to piss her off.

Grandma also said that the house needed a thorough cleaning, and that was an outright lie and a bunch of bull, because Mom and I spent hours dusting, Windexing, cleaning and vacuuming, just before she left. It was so boring and I asked Mom if she was as miserable as I was. She told me that I must have been reading her mind and that she'd rather have her fingernails pulled out with a pair of pliers than do what she was doing.

On Saturday, Grandma made me get up early and I had to help her with all the stuff that mom and I had just done. It really put me in a bad mood. I never wake up feeling all that cheerful anyway, but waking up to a dust mop, held by a woman, whom I am beginning to like less and less, is enough to ruin the whole day. I am sure glad that Mom doesn't worry about the house all that much. I felt like telling Grandma that Mom thinks that a thin layer of dust doesn't hurt anything, quite the contrary, that it protects the furniture, but I was smart and kept my mouth shut.

Before Mom and Dad left, Mom said that grandma might say something complimentary about the way the house looked and she asked me to lie to Grandma and tell her that it always looked this nice and neat. I asked Mom if she really wanted me to lie for her and she said, "No, not fib, Sam, just stretch the truth a mile. Come to think of it, what were you thinking, Helen? I am giving Grandma entirely too much credit and she'll probably spend an entire day going over everything again."

Grandma also had some things to say about the contents of our fridge and she asked me if my "mother" ever planned her meals properly. I said that, of course, they were planned with extreme care. Another untruth. Grandma is bringing the absolute worst out in me. Mom goes shopping only once a week and, every night between five and six, she opens the fridge and freezer and says, "Well now, what shall we have tonight", and within an hour we have finished dinner and done the dishes.

Grandma does one thing very well, though, and that is baking. She is also a real good cook, but she should be, because that's one of the things she really enjoys doing, besides bitching, which she does even better. She fixes cakes and pies from scratch and Dean almost ate a whole apple pie the other night. Grandma was so pleased about him stuffing himself and wanted to know if Mom ever did any baking. Dean said that she did all the time and that was another deception. We keep some ice cream in the freezer, but that's about it. When we feel like having something else, Mom or Dean runs over to the store.

I haven't mentioned Grandpa very much. He is a sweetheart and I don't know how he puts up with her. Come to think of it, she's pretty nice to him, as well she should be. He is just real quiet and ignores her most of the time and when she talks up a storm, he just keeps saying, "Yes, dear" while continuing reading the paper.

On Sunday, Dean and Grandpa went fishing. Grandma told me that we were going shopping all day, and I put my foot down and told her that Pam was coming over early in the afternoon. She said that was all right, we would just go for a short while and we did, but I hated every minute of the "short while." She had her mind set on buying a dress for me, because she was so tired of seeing her only granddaughter in jeans and t-shirts. Telling her that I would never wear the dress made absolutely no difference to her. Grandma drove Dad's car and she drives like a calcified old fart, with the seat pushed forward all the way. I tried to talk her into letting me drive, but she would not hear of it.

Anyway, when we got to the mall, Grandma wanted to go to the Woman's Shop first. She tried on many, many, dresses and finally bought one which looked just like the one she was wearing. Then we went shopping for my dress. She picked out several for me and I told her that I have chosen my own clothes for as long as I could remember, and she gave this little sneer, which I really hated. Anyway, I picked out a dress and I didn't care what it looked like on me, since I have no intention to wear it. The dress was pretty expensive and as soon as Grandma and Grandpa leave, Pam and I are going to return it and spend the money on some new jeans and whatever else we can think of. All this is made possible by Grandma being stupid enough to spend a shit load of money on this garment and having the good sense to pay cash for it.

Later that afternoon, when Dean and Grandpa got home, she wanted me to model the dress for them, but I flat refused, mainly for the simple reason that I was afraid she was going to cut the label out of it, thus making it harder for Pam and me to get our money back. Dean said that he did not do a lot of fishing, and Grandpa never touched a fishing pole, but they had the best time.

Grandpa, always so quiet, did a lot of talking and Dean thinks he is great. Grandpa just sat by the lake, smoking one cigar after another and evidently enjoyed talking to Dean.

Pam came home with me after school today and we told Grandma that I was going to spend the night at Pam's house on Friday. Grandma said, "Not so fast, Samantha. Let me check to see if this permissible" and she went to find Mom's list. When Mom talked to grandma before she and Dad left, Grandma asked her to make a list of "yeses" and "nos" of things Dean and I could or could not do. Mom was furious and told Grandma that was preposterous, but she did it anyway. Then she made another list of "yeses" and "nos" just for me and Dean to read and it was hilarious and even Dean could not stop laughing. She asked us to throw it away, but I kept it and showed it to Pam and her mom. Pam's mom was so proud of Mom and said that she could not have worded this list better. Anyway, after Grandma found out that going to Pam's was a "yes", she still insisted on calling Pam's mom to clear it with her, because, "after all, I am responsible for you while your parents are gone and, far be it for me to do anything that might upset your Dad." with the emphasis on "Dad". I had the urge to ask her, "You mean to tell me that you would not give a continental shit if you upset Mom?" but I didn't.

We quickly called Pam's mom to tell her that she could expect a call from Grandma, and then Pam and I went to Dad's study and listened in on the extension. Pam's mom said, "Oh, Mrs. Evers. What a nice surprise to hear your voice. Yes, we would love for Samantha to spend the night. She is such a delightful young lady and we always thoroughly enjoy her company." After Grandma hung up and before Pam and I put down the receiver, Pam's mom said, "And, how did I do? You two little shits hang up that phone right now." Grandma told Pam that her mother sounded like the epitome of a charming lady." We did not quite understand what she meant by that, but Pam was sure that her mom was not that.

(Later)

I just took a shower and am ready for bed. When I got out of the bathroom, Dean was sound asleep and I had to wake him up. We yelled "good night" to Grandma and Grandpa. That was good enough for Grandpa, who told us "sweet dreams", but, no, not good enough for Grandma. She wanted us to come downstairs and give her a proper hug. Dean, who never gets mad or too upset about anything, told me that she was out of her mind and why, pray tell, was a woman of advanced age, not sound asleep at one o'clock in the morning?

He didn't go downstairs and I couldn't blame him. I did and was very happy that she didn't ask me if I had brushed my teeth.

We don't really get to see Grandma and Grandpa all that much. They usually come over for Thanksgiving and only stay for a few days. I don't really mind those visits at all. Dean and I are busy and not that much around them. I have never given this much thought before, but I do feel sorry for Mom having to put up with her. I am ready for Mom and Dad to get home and to get rid of Grandma. Grandpa can stay a little longer, as far as I am concerned.

(Later)

Mom and Dad got home this afternoon and I have never been so happy in my life. They bought me and Pam the neatest pants and shirt and a leather jacket for Dean, which he has wanted for a long time. Dean even hugged Dad several times, so I guess he missed him and Mom as much as I had.

Mom said that the trip had been absolutely wonderful, but the best part was getting home and seeing her kids. Mom has her foot in a walking cast. She did something to her ankle on the last day and has to wear the cast for a few weeks. She told Grandma that the pain was relatively minor, but that the cast was a nuisance. She told me that it hurt like hell and that the cast was irritating the shit out of her.

Dad is driving his parents to the airport tomorrow and then it will be the four of us again, just the way I like it.

Dad is taking us and Pam out for dinner tonight. He also invited Pam's mom, but she declined. She told Mom that it would be entirely too stressful for her to be on her best behavior for at least an hour. God, I hope we don't see anyone I know, because the moment I say, "Hi" to someone, Grandma will probably want me to introduce her to my "nice, young friend" and I'd rather die than go through that.

❧   ❧   ❧

Sam, I almost ignored the above entry. Call it chickenshit, or whatever, but talking about Dad's mother is not something I relish doing, and, also, I feel that I have to mention my own parents, which is also not very pleasurable.

Dad and I were sorry that the visit with your grandparents did not work out all that well. You're so right. Grandpa is a wonderful man, and Dad is so much like him in many ways and fortunately he does not possess any of his mother's

highly irritating characteristics. I am sure that Grandma has many fine quali-
ties, but, at this moment, I am hard pressed to come up with any.

Years ago, Grandma went somewhere with her Garden club and Grandpa
spent a week with us. That was the first time we had ever had him over by himself and it was delightful. He is an intelligent man, a retired CPA, and he has a
fine sense of humor and is a good and loving grandfather. He doesn't shine
when he is around Grandma, who is so domineering. They are fond of each
other, though.

Dad and I were introduced to each other when we were both seniors at the
University of Texas. We dated a few times and then Dad mentioned marriage.
Think we were both a little lonely, we got along well together, and marriage
seemed like a nice idea. I know for a fact, that I was not all that much in love
with him, but then, how could I possibly not be happy with this kind, intelligent and good-looking man who treated me so well? Brian, you're going to
read this one of these days, and I know that the above paragraph will not come
as a surprise to you. You also know that it didn't take long for me to fall in love
with you and I still am and you're my whole life.

Dad's parents were living in Dallas at the time. Dad called them and told
them about us. They were anxious to meet me and invited us over for dinner,
which, Grandma said, was going to be a real "informal" get-together. This was
a great relief, since I owned few nice outfits, none of them suitable for anything
formal.

The drive from Austin to Dallas seemed very long. It was also very hot, since
the air conditioner in Dad's car did not work. Just before we got to Dallas, I
asked Dad to stop at a filling station so that I could freshen up a little and
remove the coke stain from my blouse.

My mother died of a brain aneurysm when I was in grade school. My father,
who almost solely supported the local liquor store, started drinking even more
heavily and one evening, less than a year after my mother had died, he got
more drunk than usual, got into his car and, according to the police, ran into a
huge, stationary, moving van, killing himself instantly. Hank, my older
brother, and I did not miss him. Truthfully, we were relieved. That sounds terrible, but that's the way we felt. We moved in with my father's parents and lived
with them all through high school. They were the kindest, most caring and
wonderful people one can hope for and they provided a loving home for us.
They died when Hank and I were in college and we missed them. I think of
them often and I have nothing but good memories of those years.

Sam, I am digressing. Anyway, since I had no parents, I was really looking forward to meeting Dad's and the thought that they would not like or love me at first sight never occurred to me. I had a picture in my mind of what I hoped his parents would be like. I thought that his father would be kind, gentle and quiet and that he would welcome me with open arms and I was right about all of that. I thought that his mother would be a petite lady, soft-spoken, a little plain, wearing a cotton dress that had seen better times and, of course, she would take to me instantly and Sam, was I wrong about all of that.

When Dad rang the doorbell, the door was opened by this matronly looking woman in a long evening gown, with strands of pearls around her neck and she resembled royalty without a tiara. For a fleeting moment, I was hoping that this imposing looking person was not Dad's mother, but just a house guest, kind enough to answer the doorbell, but my hopes were crushed when Dad said, "Mother, I would like for you to meet Helen." She just looked at me and I still don't know what she was thinking, or waiting for, maybe for me to curtsy and I felt so utterly unsophisticated. Then she shook my hand. Can you believe that, Sam? I also thought that if Dad and I were so fortunate to ever have any children, I would insist on them calling me "Mom" and never, ever, "Mother."

The "informal" dinner was a total disaster, at least for me. It consisted of several courses, all extremely well prepared and elegantly served, but I could not enjoy any of it, because I had to go to the bathroom again. Since I had already used it three times in a thirty-minute time span, I did not want to excuse myself again, for fear that Grandma, in my absence, would tell Dad that he, her only child, might be well advised to "court" a young lady with stronger kidneys.

The evening was finally over and I cried all the way back to Austin. Dad was a little oblivious and wanted to know why I was so upset and, a box of Kleenex later, I finally got up enough courage to tell him that I was so hurt by his mother's cold and impersonal attitude towards me. I was also convinced that Dad would replace me the next day with a more worldly person, someone his Mother would approve of. I could not wait to get back to the dorm, tell my roommate about this horrible evening and then cry myself to sleep.

Looking back, I don't think that Grandma would have approved of any girl Dad brought home, not even a young Grace Kelly, Princess Di, Ingrid Bergman or Audrey Hepburn. Since all of these ladies are dead, I should probably come up with better examples, but I cannot think of any.

Dad and I got married by a Justice of the Peace. Our witnesses were our best friends and Grandma and Grandpa were not invited. Grandma has never forgiven us for that. When we told her that we had gotten married, she immediately wanted to know if I was pregnant, and she stubbornly refused to accept the fact that I was not. I gave birth to Dean fourteen months later and it still surprises me that Grandma did not tell me that my pregnancy had been so much longer than the usual nine months.

Grandma and Grandpa came to see us right after Dean was born. Fortunately, we had a small apartment and they had to stay in a motel. When Grandma saw Dean for the first time he only weighed six pounds. She tried to ruin my proudest moment by telling Dad, in front of me, of course, "Tiny babies must run in Helen's side of the family." Then, when you were born, Sam, all eight pounds of you, she did it again: "What a gorgeous baby. She's an Evers through and through."

Over the years, we saw Dad's parents once a year, at Thanksgiving. One year, Grandma suggested that, from then on, she and Grandpa would rather spend the Christmas holidays with us and I told Dad that, if he agreed to this, I would take you and Dean and leave him and I was serious. I don't know what Dad told his mother, and I don't care. All I cared about was that they never came over for Christmas, and Dad was just as happy about that as I was.

I mentioned earlier that I could not think of anything kind to say about Grandma, but I just thought of something. She was a loving and doting Grandmother and she adored you and Dean, but she did it in such a way that it was hard for the two of you to appreciate the attention she lavished on you. And then, the nicest thing Grandma could ever have done, was to give birth to Dad.

Sam, again, I am so sorry that you were not happy being around Grandma, but a few good things came out of this visit. Evidently, you and Dean started spending some time together, and that made me happy. And what made me really feel good is the fact that you missed me so terribly much. O.K. you just missed me. That's enough for me.

When Dad took his parents to the airport, I went over to Emma's. She wrote this horribly obscene, but very humorous, message on the cast. It was so bad, even Emma said that I had better wear a sock over it on the way home. Dad read it and he laughed so hard, he had tears running down his cheeks. We searched the house for a bottle of "white out", but never found any. Dad got a can of spray paint out of the garage and painted the cast bright red.

CHAPTER 8

❀

(June)

I just read the last ten pages in this diary. They were not very interesting or entertaining, except the parts where I wrote about me, Pam and two other girls spending a few nights at Anne's lake house and about all the things we did and about how pissed Anne's parents were when they found out that we shared a beer. I never told Mom about the sip of beer, because I don't think she would have been too happy about that, but maybe I am wrong.

I also wrote a few pages about how bored I was when Pam and her sisters went to visit her dad for a week.

Anyway, last night was the greatest. Pam and I went to our first concert. *Green Day* was in San Antonio, and that is our all-time favorite group. Dad wanted to drive us, but then Dean offered and that was a lot better. Dean and a friend dropped us off after we all had a hamburger. Think they went to see a movie and then they picked us up.

Pam and I liked everything about the concert. It was the best night of our life. There were thousands of people and the noise was deafening and we loved every minute of it and now we cannot wait to go to another concert.

Dad and Mom paid for the ticket and told me that if I wanted to buy crap like posters, a T-shirt, or whatever, it had to come out of my allowance. Told Mom that, since my allowance was so piddling small, there was no way I could even afford to buy a key chain. She said that my allowance would be considerably less piddling if I did a few more chores around the house and helped Dad with yard work once in a while.

The past few weeks I did a lot of mowing. I had no idea how fast grass grows. I also washed the cars several times and cleaned the house from top to bottom. Made a lot of money, which I blew last night.

Pam never had to mow or clean or do anything to earn some extra money. When her dad took her and her sisters back to the airport, he gave each of them a hundred dollar bill. Pam thought it was just a bribe to keep them from telling their mom about his latest girlfriends, but we both decided that a hundred dollars was a hundred dollars and to hell with her dad's reasons for being so generous.

Anyway. We did not get home till after midnight and then I spent a couple of hours re-arranging my walls and I hung up all the *Green Day* posters and they look so cool. Didn't go to bed until after three, but I don't even feel all that tired today.

This summer is fun and I cannot believe I'll be a sophomore when we go back in August.

Pam and I are going to do some volunteer work in a nursing home. We start next week and we're looking forward to it. The job does not pay, but I guess that's all right. I'll get a paying job next summer when I am sixteen.

❦   ❦   ❦

Sam, when Dean was about fifteen, he mentioned one time that he would like to go to a concert. You know Dean. Never very talkative or informative and he didn't expand on the concert.

Well, when Dean said "concert", I was so pleasantly surprised, because I had no idea that Dean liked classical music. I asked him if he had a particular concert in mind, and he said that it didn't matter all that much and that I knew what he liked. I knew that he liked Country and Western but had no idea that he was also fond of classical music. I felt so proud of this versatile son.

Dean said that there was no rush, but could I please get two tickets, because he wanted to go with a friend. With a friend? You mean to tell me that not only was my son interested in this kind of music, but he even knew one other teenager who shared his passion for Beethoven and Bach. Dean never mentioned the concert again, which was so typical of him.

A few weeks later I read in the paper that some well-known symphony orchestra was going to be in Austin, so I went out and purchased some very expensive seats. After all, nothing but the best would do for my cultural and intellectual son and his friend.

I boasted to the lady at the ticket outlet that these tickets were for my son and a friend and, wasn't it encouraging that teenagers in this day and age took an interest in a symphony performance? She didn't seem impressed at all, just shrugged her shoulders and said that her children only liked hard rock. I had the insolence to tell her that her kids were missing out on a lot. All this spoken by a woman who cannot distinguish the difference between Mozart's and Brahm's music, but wish she could.

That evening at dinner, I proudly gave the tickets to Dean. I still remember the look on his face. I thought it was one of supreme delight and happiness. Dean looked at the tickets for a long time and then said very politely that this not what he had in mind. Said he and his friend wanted to listen to Willie Nelson or George Strait and I felt like a complete idiot. Guess the look on his face had not been one of delight or happiness, but one of surprise and maybe pity for his mother, who was not quite with it.

Dean explained everything to Dad and we all had a good laugh, and even I had to laugh, although not as loudly and not nearly as long as the three of you. I even told you all about all the nonsense I had told the lady at the ticket outlet and Dean said that I owed her a note of apology.

The tickets were not wasted. Dad and I went to the symphony and we loved it. Later, Dad bought season tickets and we never missed a performance.

CHAPTER 9

✿

(July)

This summer is going by in a hurry and school will start again before we know it and, probably, before I am ready for it. I really don't mind going back to school and it will be so nice to be a sophomore. Think I am going to have a tough schedule. I also want to try out for basketball.

I am really in the mood to write tonight and I want to devote some time to the Golden Years home, where Pam and I are working two afternoons a week.

We really wanted to work in a hospital, but that was not going to work out. The hospitals already had plenty of volunteers and the only place that needed help was at the other side of town and that would not be very convenient for either Mom or Pam's mother, since they would have to drive us. Golden Years home is within walking distance from where we live.

Mom and Pam's mother thought that we might find the work very rewarding, but we didn't think so at first. Smelly and depressing, yes. Rewarding, not really, at least not at first. After doing it for a few weeks, we got used to the smell and we started liking it, not the smell, but working there, and now we look forward to Monday and Wednesday afternoons.

Golden Years has about sixty rooms and each room has two beds and not very much furniture. It reminds me of a hospital in many ways, except in this place no one seems to get better.

We have to take care of the flowers, read mail to the old folks, write letters for them, listen to their life stories over and over, go around with refreshments, hand them things they cannot read, etc.

Time goes by very fast. I like reading the mail, especially to this old and almost blind lady, Mrs. Graves, who is so sweet. She gets a letter from her daughter in New Jersey every week, and it always arrives on Wednesday. Her daughter writes the shortest notes and they're all boring. The first time I read one of the letters, Mrs. Graves said very sadly, "Is that all Sylvia wrote?" and I felt so sorry for her, it made me want to cry. So the next time when I had to read that week's letter, I read it very slowly to her and I added a few words to each sentence to make it a little longer and it little more interesting, and I also changed "best wishes from Sylvia" to "all my love from your daughter." I cannot imagine writing a letter to your own mother and signing it "best wishes". I think that Sylvia is an asshole and I know I wouldn't like her if I met her. After I read the letter, I have to answer it. Mrs. Graves dictates the sweetest letters, full of lies about how happy she is and that makes me feel bad, because I cannot imagine anybody being happy in a place like this. I always have this urge to add a p.s. to the letter, something to the effect that it would be so nice and so much appreciated if she could visit her mother just once a year or so.

Going around with refreshments seems to take a long time, but it is fun. It's also the only thing that Pam and I get to do together. Something funny always happens and we have a hard time not laughing. There is one room that we would like to skip, though. A very fat lady lives in it and she spends all her time in bed. Every time we ask her what she would like to eat or drink, she says, "I cannot fink of fat until I have my teef in", and then either Pam or I (we take turns) have to go to her bathroom and pick up that nasty glass with her teeth in it. We walk to her bed very carefully, for fear of dropping or spilling it, and hand her the glass. She takes out her teeth, wipes them on her sheet and puts them in her mouth. The first time she did that, Pam whispered, "how gross" to me, but then we found out that she was not deaf. The other day she offered us some candy, the kind that was not wrapped, and she went through the candy bowl until she found some pieces she thought we would like. Pam said that it was her favorite kind, and the old lady said, "well, then eat it", but we said that we were saving it till break time. We threw it away, since we had no intention of eating anything that had been touched with the same hands as the teeth.

Pam always has to play a game of checkers with an elderly, deaf man in a wheelchair. The first time she did it, she beat him, and he got so mad he threw the checkers on the floor. Pam decided that he was a real sorry-ass loser and she always let him win from then on. You can always tell when the game is over. Pam says very loudly, "Well, what do you know, Mr. Beasly. You beat me again. Guess you're just too good for me." And that is always followed by Mrs. Green yelling, "Watch out for the old goat, Pam. He cheats."

Another man is always staring out of his window. He looks so sad and he doesn't say much. One day I made the mistake of asking him if he enjoyed living in this pretty place, surrounded by trees, He turned around very slowly and told me, "Missy, I don't give a rat's ass about all them friggin' trees. I want to be where I can see people and cars and activity. The only things moving outside this place is a bunch of squirrels screwing." I guess that answered my question.

It seems sad to Pam and me that all these people living in Golden Years are just waiting to die and it seems to us that most of them wouldn't mind if that happened any time soon. It's all very depressing. All those people have a lot of pictures of their children, grand-and great-grandchildren sitting around, but not very many of them get visitors. Mom tried to make us feel better when she said that maybe they got company on the weekends when we're not there. Sweet of you, Mom, but we don't think so.

It took me a long time to write all of this down and now I don't feel very cheerful. Told Mom that it was hard to believe that all those old people were once young and happy and, hopefully, had a lot of fun in life and look what they were reduced to now. She also said that not all elderly people age that way and that a lot of them manage to live a happy and content life, either alone or with a companion, and that Golden Years is not an indication of how all people of advanced age spend their final years. I told her that one of these years, she and Dad were going to be old and what were they going to do? She said that she hoped they would grow very old together and what were they going to do? She said skydiving, traveling the country on a Harley, swimming the English Channel, and, of course, climbing Mt. Everest, to mention only a few activities, but not until they reach their early eighties or so. I told Mom that she was full of it and she admitted that she was.

❦   ❦   ❦

Sam, Emma and I were pretty proud of you and Pam for working there all summer and for not quitting. We decided that, since you were so kind and sweet to old farts, we would never have to worry about our own old age.

We always enjoyed listening to your stories about the Golden Years residents. Even now, whenever I see a squirrel, I think about the old gentleman and I wonder why this little animal (the squirrel, I mean) would want to do something as inane or dumb like getting hit by a car, climbing a utility pole, or keeping its balance on a fence, when it could be doing something infinitely more interesting and exciting, like screwing.

Sweetheart, you did a lot of thinking that summer and you changed considerably. Your change was not a gradual process. It seemed that one night you went to bed, still wondering how far you could go before we would farm you out for a while, and the next morning you were a different person. You became a little more quiet, a lot less self-absorbed, more helpful, and more considerate of other people's feelings. Your attitude greatly improved and you also didn't argue as often as you used to. I could sum up your noticeably changed behavior in two words, but one of these is the "M" word, and I know how much you despised me for using it occasionally, well, O.K., frequently. What the heck, I'll say it anyway. You matured.

CHAPTER 10

❀

(September)

Hard to believe that we've already been in school for a month and that I am now a sophomore. I have some hard classes, but I think I'll do all right in them. I finished all my homework for tomorrow and I am going to write a little before going to bed.

I was just re-reading a lot of pages. Pam and I sure had a good time working in Golden Years. We went back there the other day to see some of the people. Most of them remembered us, but some of them didn't know us from Eve. Pam was nice enough to play a game of checkers with Mr. Beasly, that cantankerous old man. She didn't let him win this time. After they finished the game, he picked up the board, but just before he had a chance to throw it across the room, Pam thanked him profusely for teaching her the game so well and he put the board down.

Sometimes I write that nothing ever happens, but something did a few days ago and that event warrants mentioning. I finally started my period. It was about time, since I am going to be sixteen next month. Think I may be the last sophomore in my high school, or possibly in any high school in Texas, to finally start her period.

Believe me, it is nothing to get overly excited about and it is a real pain in the ass, well, in close vicinity to the ass. When I told Mom that I had started, I was so happy that she didn't say something stupid like that I was now a "woman" and no longer "her little girl". If having a period is supposed to make me feel any different, I must be missing something, because I feel the same as always. I don't even have cramps.

I asked Mom how long this was going to last and she said that it would be over within a week. She doesn't always catch on very fast, so I was more specific and asked her how many years I would be having this. She gave me the cheerful news that I will probably continue to menstruate until I am, at least, well into my forties. I asked her politely not to use the word "menstruate" again, and to just call it a "period". Well, since I am now fifteen, I have at least thirty years of this to look forward to. Not a real pleasant prospect.

Anyway, we had some pads and other unmentionables in the house, but not enough to please Mom. She went to the supermarket and came home with three bags filled with Kotex, Tampax, Feminine Deodorant spray (how utterly gross) and it looked like she had bought enough to last me the next thirty years, which was very thoughtful of her.

I used the damned pads for two days, and that was long enough, because it felt like they were shifting around, even though I was wearing my tightest underwear. I could not even concentrate in school and I could just imagine the comments on my next report card: "Due to the onset of Samantha Evers' menstrual cycle, her grades have gone down considerably."

I complained to Mom about the pads and she suggested that I try using a Tampax and I decided to go for it. She asked me if she wanted her to come in the bathroom with me, and I didn't answer her. No, Mom, of course not!!! So she gives me this huge jar of Vaseline and three boxes of different tampons, places herself outside my bathroom door and gives me instructions on how to use them. After going through a box of tampons and half a jar of Vaseline I was all greasy from the crotch (sorry, but I cannot think of another word and who cares, since I am the only one reading this diary) down. Mom told me to take a bath, relax and try again. I did and it worked and I agree with Mom, that the person who so cleverly invented the tampon should be indoctrinated in the Feminine Hall of Fame.

Let me see what else is going on. We start basketball tryouts next week and I hope I make the team. Lots of my friends are trying out and I hope I am good enough, because it's something I would really like to do.

Dean has a track meet this week-end. Think it is going to be out of town. Mom and Dad are going and they asked me to come, but I don't know if I want to do that, since it is going to be an all day event. Dean is really good and he usually comes in first or second at small meets, but this week end is a biggie and I hope he does well. Even after Dean places, he looks the same, never happy, and you wouldn't know that he had won, just by looking at him. Dean thinks that I'll make the basketball team and he told me that, once you're part of it, you have to practice every day.

Something else I would really like to do is learn to play the piano. Pam has been taking lessons for years, and she is so good. She can play anything without having to read the music. Her youngest sister is just as great. I wonder when would be a good time to bring up piano lessons to Mom and Dad. I am sure that they would mention clarinet lessons and other things I couldn't wait to start and then couldn't wait to finish right after I started them, so, maybe there is no good time to bring it up. Oh, forget it, I am too busy anyway.

Pam turned sixteen last month. She is so lucky. She can drive by herself now. Pam said that she would feel even luckier if she had something, anything, to drive, but she doesn't. They have her mother's car, but it is not very reliable. Her dad promised to buy them another car as soon as her other sister turns sixteen, but that's not until sometime next year. I am going to be sixteen next month and I cannot wait for that day.

❦   ❦   ❦

Sam, I remember your first period very well, but then, how could I possibly forget it? I went to the supermarket and overloaded one shopping cart with every possible item from the "personal hygiene" aisle. When I reached the front of the store, the assistant manager came running up and said that he would check me out on register three immediately. Poor guy. He probably thought that I had a major, female, medical problem, and that I was anemic and he didn't want me to faint in his store. Sam, I never told you, but the teenager bagging all these items was none other than one of your classmates. Didn't think you would appreciate that little tidbit of information.

Sam, give me a break. It never entered my mind to say something like you now being a "woman", etc. That's something your grandmother would say and, God help me, may I never sound like her.

You were right. Dean was a real asset to the track team and Dad and I thought that he was the best. It sometimes surprised us that Dean, who was so laid-back in many ways, was so competitive in track. He played soccer and baseball all through junior high, but he never liked it as much as track. Don't think that Dean liked team sports very much.

CHAPTER 11

✿

(October)

I had my sixteenth birthday on Thursday. The day started out great with cards, a bracelet from Mom and Dad that I wanted so badly, but didn't think I was going to get, a cool blouse from Dean, which he had bought himself and which I wore to school that day, and a present and card from Grandma and Grandpa. I felt so happy.

I could not wait for school to be out. Mom was picking me up and then we were going to the DPS building for my driver's test. I failed the damned test. I could not believe it. Evidently, I did not come to a complete stop at a stop sign and the officer took a shitload of points off for that. I told him that I had stopped, and he said that I had, but in the middle of the road and not in front of the sign. That was a load of bull. Then I got slightly nervous. When I had to make a right turn, I tried to do it perfectly, but I made it too wide and the car coming towards us had to swerve into another lane to keep from hitting me and the driver was pissed. He honked his horn and gave me the finger. Anyway, the officer started writing on his notepad again, and I knew that it was all over.

I was real upset in the car on the way home. Mom told me that she realized how much I had been looking forward to getting my license and that she was sorry that I had not passed. She also said that I could moan, groan, and bitch all the way home, but that it would be nice if I stopped all of that as soon as we got to the driveway. She said that it was, after all, my birthday, and we were all going out for dinner that night and celebrate.

I hated to tell Dean what happened, but he was real nice and said I would do better the next day.

Anyway. Dad took us and Pam out to a real nice restaurant that evening and we had the best time and I almost forgot about the stupid test. There was a piano player and a violinist. He came to our table and played "Happy Birthday" to me, at least it sounded like it. I didn't know what to do or how to look. I looked at Dad, but he looked all serious. I glanced at Dean and Pam, but they were busy looking at each other. Then I looked over at Mom, but I could not see her face, because she had most of it covered with a napkin.

Grandma called later that evening. Mom answered the phone and she listened to Grandma for a few minutes and then I heard her say that, "of course, Sam passed the test." Then I had to talk to Grandma and she sounded pretty sweet. I gave Mom a big kiss for lying to Grandma about getting my license, but she said that it was not a lie at all. Dad asked her what she meant by that. She had that it had something to do with a twenty-four hour grace period. Evidently, according to her, when the act you lied about is rectified within a day, your untruth is erased, and, since I was going to pass the test the next day, it followed that her statement to Grandma could not be constituted as a lie. Dad thanked her for clearing all that up and she gave him a big kiss.

The next day, Mom picked me up again and I passed and I was so happy and still am. Dean was home when we got back from the DPS office, so I asked Mom if I could take "our" car for a few minutes and drive to Pam's and asked her if she needed anything from the store. She said that she could always use another gallon of milk.

I drove to Pam's, picked her up, stopped at a drive-in for a shake, drove by the school to see if anybody was still playing tennis, dropped Pam off and got home an hour later without the milk. I just love to drive.

Last night, Pam and two of our friends took me out for a birthday dinner. I picked up Pam and we met Lisa and Anne in a pizza parlor. We had the best time and the jukebox was infinitely better than the violin and piano.

I am going to call it a day and go to bed.

❧   ❧   ❧

There is not a whole lot to comment on. Just one thing, Sam. After you did not pass the test, I never told you on the way home that it was permissible to "bitch". I don't quite recall how exactly how I worded myself, but I am fairly sure, albeit not entirely convinced, that the "B" word was not said out loud. On second thought, since I was undoubtedly thinking it, I might just have verbalized it.

CHAPTER 12

❊

(November)

I am going through this diary and I cannot believe that I devoted six pages to our first basketball game which we won, thanks to Sam Evers, age sixteen, who scored the last four points, which made us win the game. That was the greatest feeling. I just love basketball and always look forward to practice after school.

I am sure glad that the week is over. Don't have time to write right now, because Mom called and said that she was ready to give me a perm.

(Later)

I am sitting in my room and I think that's where I am going to stay for the rest of the week-end. Mom and Dad just went to the mall to buy some books and they wanted me to go with them, but I declined. I love going to the mall, but not tonight.

I swear that I am not going to leave this house until my hair looks better, even if it means staying home from school on Monday. My hair has always been straight and I had been bugging and begging Mom for the longest time for a soft perm and she finally agreed to it. She checked the prices in the beauty shop, thought they were entirely too high and decided to give me one herself. "After all," she said, "how difficult can it really be?" That should have given me a clue. I've heard her say that many times before and the results of whatever it is she thought she could do herself were always disastrous.

Anyway. It took Mom forever to get all the rods in, but that did not bother me at all, because we had a good time talking about all sorts of things. Several hours later, after she gave me the final rinse and after she towel dried my hair, I think that she mumbled "Oh holy shit" under her breath, but I couldn't swear to it.

Mom said that she wasn't quite finished yet and she ran to the bathroom and came back with every brush, comb, curling iron and hair dryer she could find. Then she started working on my hair, which took another thirty minutes.

Finally she said, "Sam, I have never had a martini in my life, but this might be the day to experiment" and that remark made me believe that my hair might not look all that good. Then she added, "Sweetheart, I am done now. It may look a little curlier than you wanted, but don't you worry about it. It will soften and settle down in a day or so. Please excuse me for a few minutes. I'd like to remove all mirrors from the walls" and then I knew for sure that I was going to look like shit.

I could not believe how horrible I looked. My hair was shoulder length before Mom started messing with it and ruined it. Now, with these tight curls, it barely covers my ears. Soften up in a day or so? This is going to take months. I washed my hair until we ran out of hot water and it looked even worse, which was surprising.

I did go downstairs for dinner tonight and Dean didn't say a word. When I asked him why he didn't, he said that he was sure that I didn't want to hear what he had to say and he called me "Orphan Annie". Dad did not say a word and acted as if I didn't look any different. Am sure he had strict instructions from Mom.

Mom just called me from the mall. Wanted to know if I had any plans tomorrow morning. She said that she had just talked to a beautician who could take me at ten o'clock.

(Later)

We went to the mall this morning and I had my hair done by a real nice lady. She cut my hair and did all sorts of things to it and it looks just great. Mom teased me and said that she wanted to stay for a few minutes, so that she could learn something. Don't think she ever told the lady that it was she who had given me a perm, because when the lady said that whoever had done my hair was a disgrace to her profession Mom said, "Oops. I think I hear my momma calling" and she hauled ass out of the salon.

Then Mom took me out for lunch. She said that I looked more beautiful than ever and she apologized for the horrible job she had done. I wanted to tell her that I was sorry for getting so upset with her, but I couldn't find the right words, so I just gave her a hug and told her that she was all right. Mom promised that the word "home perm" would never, ever pass her lips again.

Here I am, sixteen years old, the absolute perfect dating age. Now that I am allowed to date, I find that I am not all that interested. Cannot go out on week nights anyway, which is all right, because I am too busy with basketball and homework. By the time I get home, shower, eat dinner and do my homework, it is close to eleven and I am ready to go to bed.

A couple of weeks ago, I wrote about going to the movies with Alan and him holding my hand in the theater and that I didn't think it was all that I had dreamed of. He is a nice guy, but just a friend. He keeps calling me to go out again, so once in a while, when there's nothing better to do on Saturday night, we'll go out. We usually go with some other kids from school and that's really a lot of fun—better than me being by myself with him and running out of things to talk about.

Dean finally had a date the other night. He took a girl out for a hamburger and a movie. Way to go, Dean, you know how to show a girl a good time. He hasn't mentioned her since. I kinda want to ask him if he's taking her out again, but Mom told me not to bug him, but if I happened to find out she'd like to know.

❧   ❧   ❧

Yes, that first basketball game was something. I had a lump in my throat when, after the game, your team members came running up to you and I will never forget that happy look on your face. You were a good player, Sam, and an asset to the team. Your coach told me one time that you were not the best player on the team, but that your speed and enthusiasm made up for it. I never quite understood what she meant by "it".

Sam, I did an appalling job on your hair. Dad always accused me of never reading the instructions on anything, but I did read them on the "you-know-what" and I followed them closely. I don't remember how much I tipped the beautician, but I am sure it was an exaggerated amount. Worth every penny.

CHAPTER 13

❀

(November)

Pam and I went to our first funeral yesterday. Neither one of us wanted to go, but we were more or less forced into going by our mothers.

"Cabbage Patch" Irma's father died unexpectedly. Nobody likes her. She is fat, has greasy hair, is not very friendly and she hangs around with two other girls who look just like her and who are just as unpopular.

Mom said that, since Cabbage Patch did not have that many friends, this should be one more reason to go. I asked her what the other reason was, and she said "compassion." I still did not want to go, but it got me out of school for a couple of hours. Mom said that she and Emma were going for a variety of reasons, but she did not expand. Think that Pam's youngest sister and Cabbage Patch take piano lessons from the same teacher.

Mom and Pam's mother picked us up after second period and we all went to the Presbyterian church for the service. There were not a whole lot of people and only a handful of kids from school, so, in a way, I am glad I went.

The worst part came after the service. We stood in line to give our condolences to the family and Pam and I noticed that everyone gave Cabbage Patch a hug. I asked Pam if she was going to do that and she said she would, but only if I would set the example. I gave Cabbage Patch a quick, a very quick, hug, but Pam did not. She later said that my hug was long enough for the both of us.

Pam's mother and Mom really made us mad in church. Even Pam, who never says anything bad about her mom, wanted to make her disappear. They were sitting in the back by themselves and all of a sudden we heard this noise. Pam and I turned around very slowly and there they were, with their head on their chest, wiping their eyes with a tissue. Now, wasn't that hypocritical? Pam and I didn't think that either one of them knew Cabbage Patch's father and they were sitting there, crying.

Cabbage Patch was back in school today and I felt a little sorry for her. After all, she lost her father and that must be terrible. I know how I would feel if anything ever happened to Dad. Don't think I would ever get over it. I heard from some kids at lunch that Cabbage Patch did nothing but cry all morning, and she also cried about not having her homework. Of course, none of the teachers expected her to be prepared. Come to think of it, I heard that she never does her homework, so the teachers were probably thinking, "What else is new?" when she did not have her homework. She is pretty stupid.

Last year, Cabbage Patch wanted to try out for cheerleader and all the boys told her that she should, because she had a good chance to make the cheerleading team. She never caught on to the fact that they were just making fun of her. I told Mom about that and she got furious. She said that it was very unkind and mean to make fun of a person who is not endowed with a lot of brains. I asked her if she ever made fun of other kids when she was in school and she said that she had. Mom volunteered entirely too much information, but I remember her saying that she had been just as inconsiderate and unfeeling a teenager as we are nowadays and that, looking and thinking back, there were a lot of things that she had said or done and that she later deeply regretted. Be that as it may, I don't think that I will ever regret not liking Cabbage Patch, but I hate myself for not feeling more sorry for her.

I would really like to watch TV for a while, but I have too much homework. Mom said that she had not used the oven in a long time and that it was time she baked something, lest she forgot how it works, so she baked brownies. They are delicious. Mom ate three of them and is now punishing herself by running in place for thirty minutes, ten minutes for each brownie. Don't know why she bothers. She's not fat at all and Dad sometimes tells her that he doesn't understand why she's so concerned about her weight. I eat all the time, but never gain anything. I weigh 101 lbs, just like about a year ago. Mom said that her average weight, give or take ten pounds or so, is 115. I saw her step on the scale once, right after she got out of the shower and I asked her how much she weighed. Now, get this nonsense. She said that she weighed approximately so many pounds, but that she did not know her exact weight yet, because she still had to make allowances for wet hair, insufficient toweling off, her bracelet, necklace and wedding ring, the time of day and the fact that she had not shaved her legs. I figured that she had gained a few pounds.

❧   ❧   ❧

Sam, I didn't want to go to the funeral either, but I was sucked into going by Emma, who said that there nothing as rewarding as a good friendship. I couldn't figure that one out, but Emma said that it boiled down to me having to go with her.

Nobody knew much about Cabbage Patch's family. Later we heard stories about how Cabbage Patch's father had abused his wife and children for years and Emma said that having a heart attack and dropping dead was probably the only thoughtful thing the S.O.B. had ever done for his family.

Oh Honey, Emma and I were not crying in church that day. When the minister got to the part where he elaborated on what a wonderful husband, father and provider the deceased (Earl) had been, Emma leaned over to me and whispered, "Helen, listen to me carefully. Don't believe a word the minister is saying. Earl, that little mother, used to hang around our neighborhood, looking for odd jobs, and he gave everybody the creeps. The police couldn't do anything about it, so old Mrs. Post from down the street reassured everyone at a block meeting that she would take care of him and she did. She bought a B.B. gun and next time Earl came around, she shot him in the knee. Then she apologized to the whole neighborhood for not being more accurate, since she had been aiming for his balls." I quickly looked away from Emma and thought about famine, incurable diseases, earthquakes and other catastrophes to keep a straight face, bit it did not work. Sam, I am ashamed to say that, what you referred to as crying, was nothing but uncontrolled and inappropriate laughter by two women who behaved badly and yes, very immaturely. Later that day I told Emma that her timing for this story had been a little off, but she did not feel that way. She said, "Church is a place for honesty, Helen.", whatever that meant. I also asked Emma why she had dragged me to this funeral, and her reply was, "Admit it, Helen. You had a good time."

After Dean got home that day he said that a lot of trashy boys like to take Cabbage Patch out. He said that they were not attracted to her brain (she didn't have one), or her looks (also non existent), but to a lower part of her body, the "crotch area" as Dean called it. I wanted to tell Dean that there are ways and ways of describing parts of the body and that there was probably a very nice, less offensive, synonym for "crotch area", but I didn't. That was about the longest sentence Dean had uttered in a long time, and I was not about to criticize any part of it.

Sam, why did everyone call Irma "Cabbage Patch"? I don't remember if you ever told me. Truthfully, I don't care. I have no idea what happened to Irma and I don't remember if she ever graduated. Again, I don't care.

CHAPTER 14

※

(December)

Tomorrow is Dean's eighteenth birthday, He does not act at all excited about it and said that it just another day. He is so difficult to buy for. I asked him a couple of weeks ago what he would like for his birthday and he said that he would be happy with anything. Thank you, Dean. That limits it considerably.

I got him a subscription to a boring hunting and fishing magazine, but I really didn't like that gift all that much, so yesterday I went shopping and bought him a good looking shirt and a funny, and pretty dirty, birthday card. Dad bought him a shotgun and Mom hates it. She doesn't like guns or knives. Dad said that when he bought Dean his first pocketknife, Mom went outside and dulled it on a brick.

Last week, Dean went to the post office and registered for the Selective Services, which almost had Mom in tears. She told Dad that she would be the first one to encourage Dean to fight when our country is invaded, but she is opposed to him being sent to some godforsaken country that she can neither pronounce nor find in the atlas, to fight for a cause nobody can understand or justify. Said she'd move us all to Canada first before she would let that happen. She said that since Dean was such a non-violent and laid back-person, he would probably be one of the first casualties and she didn't want one of his commanders presenting her and Dad with a U.S. flag at his service. Dean told her that she had no choice in the matter and that, of course, it would be an American flag. She really got on her soap box. Dad tried to calm her down, but he was not very successful.

Mom and I had a long talk the other day about all sorts of things and Mom mentioned that she was going through a difficult stage in her life and I immediately said "menopause?" She laughed and said that she still had that to look forward to. She was referring to parenthood. It was a long speech, but one of her better and less tedious ones, so I am going to write it down.

Mom said that a parent starts teaching her or his child to be self sufficient, independent, mature and honest from an early age on. At times it seems that you, as a parent, are making absolutely no progress. Then, suddenly, you wake up to the realization that your child has succeeded in achieving all the goals you had set out for him or her. You feel immensely proud of your child, but this pride is somewhat overshadowed by the fear that you are going to lose this young adult. Mom added that the years seem to go by too fast and she thinks that Dean and I have reached so many goals and her mind has a hard time absorbing all of that. I think I am screwing up part of Mom's soliloquy, but I am sure about the general gist. She feels that Dean and I are growing up too fast and she's probably beginning to feel old. I must be getting somewhat more mature, because I was wise enough not to mention the part about her age to her.

Years ago, when I still lost my temper pretty often and got mad at the slightest thing, I often wrote in my diary that Mom could be a real bitch for not letting me do something or other. She always gave me a logical explanation, at least she thought it was, but I never could accept it. Think we're getting along a lot better. What do you know, Mom is finally maturing.

Pam is dating some and I wish I were, but my dates are few and far in between. Mom said that you cannot force certain things in life and that, one day, I will meet someone who likes me as much as I like him. Hope that day gets here soon. I asked Mom about her dates when she was going to school. She said that she dated off and on in high school and college, but that it was more off than on. Said she never met anyone whose signature she practiced. Then she met Dad at a party. They spent the entire evening together and when she got back to the dorm, she wrote "Helen Evers" on all her notebooks and she knew they were going to get married. Then Dad did not call her for a week and she got all concerned, because she was anxious to get started on the wedding plans. She said that she and Dad are going on twenty years of marriage and that she never knew the true meaning of happiness until she married Dad and had two children. I asked her if she ever looked at other men, just for the hell of it, and she said that, of course she did, and she knew that Dad looked at other women, but that's where it stopped. Said she had the best and that Dad had the very best. Oh Mom, you can be so full of shit.

✤   ✤   ✤

Sam, Dad often had to calm me down and I sometimes got so tired of him telling me to "cool my jets" and wished he would come up with a different expression or just tell me to shut the fuck up. Sorry about that. As you may have gathered, I just came back from Emma's.

Sam, did I really tell you that I sometimes looked at other men? I must have, or you wouldn't have written it down. Well, haven't done any looking in a long while, so I may just do a little of that tomorrow or so, when I go for a walk. Just kidding.

I believe that the main reason for having chosen the above passages is that you finally admitted that one of my speeches was truly fantastic. O.K. You didn't exactly classify it as such, but isn't "better and less tedious" synonymous with "truly fantastic"? I am so sure it is, I don't even have to consult Webster's.

CHAPTER 15

❀

(January)

This is the first day of the new year. Guess I should really make some resolutions, but I cannot think of anything. I asked Dean if he had made any resolutions, and he said that he didn't think so. Come on, Dean, either you have or you haven't. Mom said that she had made a couple, but that she wasn't going to share them with me. She was afraid that if she didn't stick to them, I would rub it in. Of course I would. Dad said that he was perfect and couldn't think of anything to improve himself. Mom said she could and wanted to know if he was interested in hearing about them, but he wasn't.

Anyway. We never go anywhere New Year's eve, because, according to Mom, that is just one of the nicest family nights, and best spent at home. We snacked all evening, watched TV, played cards, had a fire in the fireplace, and had to wake Mom up just before midnight. So much for "best family night". We had invited Pam and her family, but their grandmother is visiting and Pam's mother didn't want us to put up with her. Mom said that she didn't mind at all, because if she could tolerate, although barely, Loretta (our Grandma) for five days, she could put up with anybody for one evening. I don't think I was supposed to hear that telephone conversation. Pam's mother decided to stay home anyway.

Cannot believe school starts again tomorrow. I am looking forward to it. With the exception of Pam, I haven't seen a lot of my friends. This Christmas vacation was absolutely fantastic. Dad, Mom, Dean and I went skiing in Steamboat Springs and we had a blast. We were in Colorado once before, but that was in the summer and it was hot and not nearly as pretty as it was with all the snow. I would not mind living there. We only stayed one week and got home Christmas eve.

We left early on Saturday morning. Flew out of San Antonio into Denver and the flight was great. Dad flies all the time, but Dean and I have only flown twice before. We love it. I was sitting next to Mom on the plane, which was the pits. Dean and Dad were sitting two rows in front of us. As soon as we landed I asked Dad if I can have the seat next to him on the way back, since Mom is just no fun.

I never realized before how much Mom hates flying. She sat down, fastened her seatbelt, gave me a note and closed her eyes. A note? It read: "Sweetheart, do me a big favor. Do not talk to me, unless it is to inform me that we have landed safely at the right airport. Do not walk up and down the aisle, because the movement might make the plane rock. Do not try to be funny by inform-ing the stewardess that I am an alcoholic when I order three Bloody Mary's right after take-off. Do not comment on my hands being folded in prayer when I am not holding on to a Bloody Mary. And, do not tell me that flying through air pockets is almost as fun as being on a roller coaster. I love you." Cannot believe she went through all that trouble. Dad checked on us one time and wanted to know if Mom was comatose.

As soon as we landed, Mom ran off the plane and, in front of thousands of people, she totally embarrassed me and Dean by getting down on her knees and saying, "Thank you, thank you, dear God." loud enough for the entire air-port to hear. Even Dean looked surprised and asked her what the heck she was doing. She said that during the entire flight she had been praying for a safe flight and landing and she thought that the least she could do was thank God for keeping his promise. Dean agreed, but wanted to know why she had to do it out loud and on her knees, and Mom said that it was more meaningful that way. Dad just smiled and told me and Dean, when we were waiting for our lug-gage and Mom was in the bathroom, that thanking God on her knees was nothing compared to some of the things she has done after a safe landing, but he would not elaborate, which was just fine with Dean and me. He did say, though, that Mom has written him hundreds of notes over the years and that he has kept every one of them. Some of them didn't make any sense, he said. One night, on his way home from a business trip, his plane was delayed, so he called Mom and told her he would not be in till much later. When he got home, there was a note waiting for him on the kitchen table. It read: "Honey, please wake me up when you get home, so that I can stop worrying about you."

Dad said that since Mom was snoring loudly, he didn't think that she was all that worried and he did not wake her up.

We stayed in a real nice lodge. It had two bedrooms, a bathroom and a kitchen, which Mom refused to use. Dean and I shared a room and I saw him in his thermal underwear, which was not a pretty sight. We had a lot of fun together, though.

Mom and Dad had skied before, and did not need to take any lessons. Dean and I signed up for a morning class and it was great. We learned quite a lot in two days. Dean caught on faster than I did and he helped me quite a bit. The ski instructor was awesome and a big flirt. Dean thought he was a sissy, but what does he know. We skied the easy and intermediate trails and did pretty good.

We met a lot of nice people, mostly from the east coast and we did quite a few things together. O God, I can sound so much like Mom, it scares me. Had our lesson in the morning, skied all afternoon, played cards and pooped out early. A lot of girls seemed to like Dean and kept asking me about him. Think it pissed them off that he didn't pay a lot of attention to any of them.

We skied with Mom and Dad a few times. Dad is fantastic, very sure of himself and he never falls. Mom is fast, also very sure of herself, but she falls a lot. She really is not very graceful. Dad said she is too pigeon-toed. That was the best vacation ever. Wish we could go back next year.

It was nice to get home Christmas eve, light the tree, make a fire in the fireplace, and pretend to be interested when Mom read *Twas the Night Before Christmas* like she does every year. 'Twas nice to do that when we were little, but not any more. Asked Mom when she was going to stop that pretty annoying tradition and she said, "not until senility sets in". I also called Pam and we talked for a long time.

Didn't do much the rest of the time. Pam and I just hung around and had a good time.

❦   ❦   ❦

Sam, Dad evidently told you and Dean that I've done some pretty strange things after landing. I've been racking my brain, but I cannot recollect anything. It couldn't be my hugging the pilot or writing a Thank You note to the airlines because, after all, everyone does that. Dad just got home and I asked him. He came up with several occurrences, but they were all so minor in importance that I am not going to waste my valuable time by writing them down.

Yes, Dad is an excellent skier. His parents used to take him to Colorado every year. Believe it or not, your Grandpa used to be an expert and he taught Dad and did it well. I am sure you can also believe that Grandma never ventured out on the slopes. She probably stayed back in the cabin or motel, close to the First Aid kit with the telephone on her lap, ready to dial the ski patrol in case her "two boys" were not back the minute they were supposed to be. Sam, sometimes I really dislike myself intensely for speaking so negatively about your grandmother, but I cannot help myself. She brings out the worst in me.

Brian, Honey, I refuse to take notice of the remark you made about my feet, because you are absolutely correct, but I cannot ignore your comment on my sleeping habits. I do not snore.

CHAPTER 16

✿

(February)

I just read through everything I wrote since January 1, and it was not much. It must have been a slow month.

Dad had his birthday yesterday. Every year we do the same for him, which is not a whole lot. He gets the usual cards, birthday cake, books and shirts, all so very boring. Mom decided that it would be nice to do something special for Dad this year, something memorable. Dean or I could not think of anything unusual, and Mom could not either. Then Pam's mother got involved. She said that sending a stripper to Dad's office on his birthday and having her sing "Happy Birthday" would definitely stand out in his memory for years to come. Dean and I did not think Dad would like that at all, but Pam's mother convinced us all.

Mom called the office and talked to Evelyn, his secretary. She checked his schedule and, on his birthday, he had a meeting with the City Planning Committee or whatever in his office. Mom told Pam's mother that maybe we should forget the whole idea, but Pam's mother would not hear of it. She said that sending a stripper to Dad's office while he was in a meeting with a bunch of old farts might brighten up his day and also, it would be something extremely personal to share with his grandchildren years from now. Mom bought it.

Anyway. Mom and Emma got on the phone and they found a place in San Antonio that advertised party goods and strippers for all occasions. They drove to San Antonio to check out the place and got it all arranged. Dean wanted to know what kind of "chick" Mom and Emma had chosen. Mom showed us a picture of her and she looked old and not at all pretty. She looked almost as bad as some those women on a calendar I saw in that gift shop where I had bought Dean's birthday card. Dean thought that she was pretty fugly. Mom asked what that meant and Dean acted like she should know that it was "fucking ugly". Mom said that seemed like a useful word to know and she said she would try to incorporate it in her conversations. Mom told us that the stripper would get there about half an hour after the meeting started. Dean asked her what something like that cost, and Mom said it was not very much.

Yesterday morning, Mom chickened out and called the agency to cancel, but it was too late and she wouldn't get her money back, so she decided to go ahead with it. She thought that Dad would appreciate the joke. Dean and I were not so sure. When Dean and I got home from school yesterday, Mom looked a little concerned and said that Dad had not called yet.

Dad got home around six that evening and he never mentioned a thing. Mom had fixed him a real nice dinner. We were beginning to think that the stripper had not shown up. Mom asked him after we had eaten if anything out of the ordinary had happened at the office that day. Dad finally said that he was not too happy about this woman stripping down to almost nothing and singing "Happy Birthday" off key. Mom wanted to know where his sense of humor was.

Grandma called Dad that evening. I answered the phone and she wanted to know if we had done anything special for "my Daddy". ("My Daddy"? How old does Grandma think I am.). I told her that we had, but I wanted Dad to be the one to tell her. Dad got on the phone, talked to her for a few seconds and then he told her about the birthday surprise and he laughed. Mom was surprised that he told his mother.

Well, I think that Dad thought it was pretty funny after all. Mom had better watch out, though, because I am sure he is going to get even on her birthday. I wonder how old Mom is? Seems she has been thirty-five for many years now.

❦   ❦   ❦

Sam, until this day I don't understand how we could have let Emma talk us into it. I had already told her that Dad always sounded like a pompous ass when I happened to call him while he was in a meeting, and how would he react when one of his meetings was interrupted by a stripper? Emma reassured me that he would just love it. She said that she always enjoyed Dad's sense of humor and that he would treasure this day for years to come. Oh, Emma, you are so bad and I was so dumb for listening to you.

Emma came over later that evening and Dad told us that his meeting had been postponed until the next week. Emma said that was the biggest disappointment of her life, because she had been looking forward so much to Dad describing the look on the old geezer's faces when the woman sashayed in.

I know that Dad never told his mother about this horrible surprise. Sam, how can I be so sure? Because I never got a note from Grandma, telling me that I had vulgar taste. I think he related the whole event to Grandma after she had already hung up the phone.

Truthfully, that whole birthday thing for Dad was a big mistake on my part. The fact that he didn't enjoy it very much did not bother me at all. What saddened me was the stripper, a woman old enough to be a youngster's grandmother, a woman who had reached an age where she has finished raising her kids and should enjoy life instead of having this rather degrading job. I made the mistake of telling all this to Emma. All she said was, "For Christ's sake, Helen. How do you know she even had any kids? And what makes you think that she doesn't like what she's doing?" That didn't make me feel any better. We had already paid the agency in advance, but I didn't care and sent another check made out to this lady to the agency with a note thanking her for her wonderful performance which was so much appreciated by my husband. That made me feel a little better. I never told Emma about that.

Sam, I am trying to think how old I was at that time. I believe that I was, indeed, thirty-five and I did not have another birthday until Dean's sophomore year in college.

CHAPTER 17

❀

(February)

Today I went to a garage sale in the basement of some church. We had a call a few weeks ago from someone who wanted to know if we would like to rent a space to sell all our old junk. A couple of days ago I started cleaning up my room and found a lot of stuff I would not mind selling. Mom also asked Dean to go through his room, but he couldn't find anything he wanted to get rid of. Either that, or he was too lazy. He saves everything and his room is crammed, but it looks neat and organized, not like my room, which is always a mess, even right after I clean it up, which doesn't happen too often.

Mom asked Dad to go through the garage, but he refused because he hates garage sales. Mom told him that 10% of the proceeds will go to a local animal shelter, but that was not enough incentive for him.

Mom found a lot of things in the house that she no longer needed or wanted. Then we decided to go in the attic and see what we could find. Cleaning the attic was a lot of fun. I found the dress Mom got married in. She took off her blouse and tried it on and it still fit and that made her happy. I told her that it wasn't all that nice. She said it looked good when she wore it without sneakers and jeans. Then I tried it on and I asked Mom how I looked. She didn't say a word. Just looked at me and gave me a hug and told me she loved me.

Mom is as bad as Dean is and cannot throw anything away either. There were two huge boxes filled with stuffed animals and I was ready to get rid of them all. We sorted them all out and sorting out to Mom means looking at them for a long time, talking about where they came from and then putting them back in the box. There were at least fifty stuffed animals and dolls, and we are only getting rid of one of them, a pink alligator. Mom said that there is an unwritten garage sale law which prohibits you from selling certain items. I'll write some of them down. You cannot sell (1) things you used to be fond of, (2) objects received from grandparents and relatives whether you liked them (the presents) or not, (3) toys given to a child under the age of five and, (4) anything stuffed when you distinctly remember the age of your child when he or she received it. Well, needless to say, no matter what I found, we couldn't get rid of it because it fit one of those categories.

There were a lot of books and we're selling all of those. Also found a lawn-mower, a tiller and several tools. Since the tools were in the attic, Mom did not think that Dad had any use for them, but, just in case, she thought it wise if we didn't tell him anyway. Also found Mom's and Dad's first dining room set and that, of course, we're keeping for Dean when he has his own apartment. There were three trunks with blankets, sheets and pillows that we're getting rid of and four old suitcases without locks. Also a cute tricycle that Dean and I used to ride.

All in all, we found a lot of things. Dean carried everything downstairs and put it in the garage, and Mom covered up some of the things, such as Dad's tools, etc. with some old sheets. She said that Dad was not very observant, but, just in case he surprised her, she wanted to be on the safe side. Then the three of us put price tags on everything. I added it all up and, if we sold everything, we might make as much as $ 500.00, which sounded like a lot of money for junk we didn't want anymore. Mom said she would keep 2/3 and Dean and I could divide the remaining 1/3. I think my share should be larger, since Dean did not help us a whole lot.

I spent a lot of time at the sale today. Dean came only for a minute or so. He got bored. I had a good time looking at everyone else's crap and found a few things I wanted to buy, but I didn't. There were about ten other people who had rented space and I saw a lot of kids I knew. Think that Mom was doing pretty good selling all her stuff. I asked her if she was having a good time and she wanted to know if it was time to go home yet. Guess the answer was "no".

We have been home for a while now and Mom is still figuring out how much we made. All right. She just gave me and Dean $30.00 each and said that she was sorry that it was less than we had hoped for. She also said that she never wants to hear the words "garage sale" again.

❧   ❧   ❧

Sam, that sale sounded like such a good idea at the time. I always thought that the purpose of a garage sale was to get rid of unwanted items and make a little money, and I probably could have, had it not been for certain circumstances. The lady sitting next to me was selling a brand new punch bowl set. I thought that my life would not be complete unless I owned a set, so I bought it. Sam, it is still brand new and yes, still sitting in the attic. I also purchased an electric chainsaw for Dad, the kind that only cuts branches not exceeding 1/4" in diameter. Think Dad used it once and it is now keeping the punch bowl company.

By the time I had made a contribution to the church, bought two raffle tickets and four boxes of girl scout cookies, paid for your and Dean's lunch, picked up a take-out dinner for four, after all, how could I possibly prepare a meal after this exhausting afternoon, I had spent approximately a hundred dollars, and that was quite a lot more than I had made.

The minister was an extremely nice and charming man, who seemed genuinely interested in the mower, tiller and books. I thought that lightning might strike me on the way home if I charged this devout man even the slightest amount, so I donated all these items to his church. A family was in need of blankets and sheets. I felt sorry for them, so you can guess how much I charged them. Nothing.

I did sell some miscellaneous items and made a grand total of forty-six dollars and some change, a far cry from the five hundred dollars we were hoping to make. Ten per cent of the proceeds went to the animal shelter. I did not think that four dollars and sixty cents could do a whole lot for the shelter, so I donated the entire amount. It doesn't take a Rhodes scholar to figure out that it was not a profitable afternoon.

Sam, I always thought that Dad and Dean were so much alike, not just in character, but also in looks. You resembled me in personality, but I always thought that you didn't look like either me or Dad, until that day in the attic when I saw you standing there in my old dress. You may not like to hear this, Sam, but you looked like me and I felt that I was seeing myself in a twenty year old mirror and I thought, once again, about time going by so quickly and about Dean and you going off to college before we knew it and before we'd be ready and about how much Dad and I would miss you both.

CHAPTER 18

❀

(March)

Last week I wrote about how concerned I was about the test I took in Spanish, but I made a 90 on it. Think that Miles had to curve our grades a little. The only grade higher than mine was Jose's, but he doesn't count, since he is from Mexico. Don't know why he is taking that class, maybe for an easy A. Every time Miles explains something about grammar or whatever, Jose interrupts and corrects him. Pretty irritating. Am sure that Miles hates his guts. He's beginning to ignore Jose and we cannot blame him. He's on the track team with Dean and, according to Dean, he's pretty good. Jose is kinda good looking in a sissy way and pretty damned stuck on himself and he's always combing his hair. He thinks that all the girls are madly in love with him, but I got news for him. He has the crappy habit of putting his arm around a girl and saying, "Como esta, muchacha." He did that to me the other day and I told him, "Fuck off, amigo." Then he said a lot in Spanish. Didn't understand a word of it, but that's probably just as well. I told Mom what I told Jose and she said that was kind of a crude comeback. Pam's mother was at our house and she said, "Way to go, girl. I couldn't have worded it better myself." Pam's mom is so much fun.
 A couple of weeks ago, when we were cleaning out the attic, we found a trunk with a lot of boxes in it, all filled with pictures. Mom said that we didn't have time to look at them, but would do so some other time.
    When I got home from school today, Mom was sitting in the middle of the living room with millions of pictures around her. She had bought a dozen photo albums and was in the process of sorting out pictures. Dad is in Dallas for a few days and she thought this was a good time to get some things done. Mom and Dad keep some albums in their bedroom and all the pictures on the

floor were just miscellaneous photos she never bothered to put in albums. I bet you anything that she won't put one picture in any of the albums. I helped her for a while and it was fun. Think I started bugging her, because she asked me if I had any homework. Then, when I went upstairs she called me every five minutes or so to look at some picture I just had to see.

Some of those pictures were funny. I found one of her and Dean in the hospital, right after he was born. Mom looked just like she does now, except younger. I showed her the picture and she went on and on about what a precious baby Dean was and also that was the only time she ever had any boobs to speak of. I told Mom that her sentence structure left much to be desired and she said that she didn't give a shit. Mom, your language also leaves much to be desired.

Also found some pictures of Mom in college, wearing long skirts and socks and I thought she looked pretty dumb. Mom must have been reading my mind. She said that, years from now, my children will look at pictures of me when I was in college and think the same thing that I was thinking of Mom.

I also found a picture of Mom and this pretty good looking and very muscular guy. She said that she only had a blind date with him. When I asked her why she didn't have any more dates with him, she gave me one of her strange answers. She said that he was very much into weight lifting and that she made it a rule never to date any man whose breasts were bigger than hers more than once. I told Mom that he had more than likely dumped her and she admitted that he had.

Then there were a lot of pictures of this little boy with glasses and very short hair, wearing overalls. I asked Mom who that geeky kid was. Mom looked at those pictures for the longest time and then said that this little nerd grew up to be a smart and handsome man, a wonderful and loving husband and a great father, "Yours, Sam." So sorry, Mom. Not too long ago, I asked Mom why she had fallen in love with Dad. Just then, Dad came in from working in the yard. He was wearing a pair of cut-offs and he looked all sweaty and he smelled and Mom said that this was not the right time to ask her that question, but then she hugged him anyway.

There were also some pictures of Mom's parents, but she didn't say too much about those. Think she got a little sad when she saw them. Mom was wondering what to do with all those pictures of people who had died, her parents, grandparents, some aunts and uncles, a few friends and some people that Dad must have known, because she didn't recognize them. I suggested to her that we start an album and put all those dead people in it, but Mom said that was terribly morbid and she did not like the idea at all. When I asked her what she was going to do with all those pictures, she suggested that we put them all back in the box and that's just what I thought she would say. Don't know why I even asked.

There was a pile of pictures on the floor that Mom was going to throw away. I took them all and she said I could take as many photo albums as I wanted. I asked Dean if he wanted me to organize an album for him and he said "whatever", so I decided that since he didn't care, I wasn't going to waste my time on him. Mom said that whenever Dean says "whatever", it means that he cares, so she asked me to go ahead and make an album for him. I am glad she can figure him out.

❀   ❀   ❀

Sam, I really don't know exactly why I chose the above passage. It certainly wasn't to tell you that I never took the time to put any of those pictures in an album, because you probably already knew that.

Sam, since Dean wasn't very informative, it was, like you said, not easy to figure him out or read his mind. He was a sweetheart, an easy teenager and eager to please. The times Dad and I had to come down on him were few and far between, and he never repeated his mistake. One time we found out that he had been driving and drinking a beer, which did not please us at all. Dad tried to talk to him, but Dean was not very responsive. When Dad asked him if he had made any sense, Dean just said, "Yeah, guess so. It won't happen again." and, as far as we know, it never did. Dad and I were not against drinking and we enjoyed an occasional glass of whatever whenever we went out for dinner but we only kept a bottle of Scotch in the house, mainly for Emma, who made such a wonderful production out of sipping a small glass. Any more than that in our home would have reminded me of our kitchen cabinets when I was growing up. They were overflowing with bottles, frequently replaced with a new supply and all consumed by my father, who must have drunk enough for the entire adult population in the state of Texas.

After Dad had that talk with Dean, he bought some beer, stuck it in the fridge and told Dean he could help himself, just as long as he was not going to drive after consuming one. It sat there for at least a year and I finally opened one and washed my hair with it.

Just one more thing. Sam, you were vocal, you made your opinions very clear and we always knew when and why you were upset. As hard as this sometimes was on our nerves, it was still easier to deal with than Dean's silent behavior.

CHAPTER 19

❀

(May)

I am at our neighbor's house, babysitting the Myers' girls. They are pretty sweet, especially when they're sound asleep. Susie, the oldest, is almost five and Amy is two. Their parents don't go out until after they have fed and bathed them, so I really don't have to do a whole lot and it is an easy job. Think this is my fourth time to babysit and I like it and it is easy money.

Mrs. Myers is quiet and her husband talks even less and he never says a word to me when they leave, but when they get home he cannot stop talking and he smells of beer and cigarettes and it makes me want to puke. The last time I babysat, I was only there for four hours and they owed me eight dollars. He gave me a twenty dollar bill and told me to "keep the change, honey" and I didn't like the way he said that. He makes me feel a little uncomfortable.

Susie is so sweet. She talks all the time, asks one question after another and never waits for an answer."Sam, where did you get your dark hair? Why are you older than me? How come you get to stay up after we go to bed? Why are you chewing gum?"

For tonight, Mrs. Myers had checked out a Walt Disney video, a cartoon. I thought I would be bored, but I wasn't. Every time we watched a good part, Susie wanted me to rewind it. Amy just at on my lap sucking on her thumb and she never made a sound. Once in a while, she took her finger out of her mouth, pointed at the TV and sighed. She is so cuddly and she smells so good. When the movie was over, she said, "bed" and that was the first thing she had said all evening.

They had to go to bed around nine, but Susie wasn't ready. She said that she never went to sleep until midnight, but I'd heard that before and didn't pay any attention. Finally got them in bed and read a Dr. Seuss story. They seemed to like it, but when I finished the book, Susie said that Amy hated that story and she wanted me to read another one, just to make her sister happy, so I did. After I turned out their light, Susie yelled that I had forgotten to give her a Coke and that she couldn't sleep unless she had a sip. Had heard that before too, so I gave her a sip of water and she mumbled that would have to do.

The Myers' won't be home until around one o'clock, so I have plenty of time to write in my diary. At eleven I am going to watch an R-rated movie on cable. Hope it has a lot of sex in it. Shit, I just checked the TV guide more carefully and it is only rated R for violence and strong language, but absolutely no mention of sex. Now, doesn't that beat all. I hate violence, could care less about language, so I may as well forget it and watch something else instead.

Would really like to call Pam and find out what she is doing, but I'd better not use the phone, just in case Mrs. Myers calls to find out if everything is going all right. I am going to Pam's tomorrow evening anyway and will talk to her then. She has invited five friends and we're going to check out movies, eat pizza, listen to all our favorite music and spend the night. It will be a helluva lot of fun, kind of a slumber party. I had a slumber party years ago, when I was in sixth or seventh grade. Don't remember who all showed up, besides Pam, but we had a great time. The next day I asked Mom when we could have another one. Don't remember what her answer was, but "When pigs fly, honey" comes to mind.

I just checked on Amy and Susie and they're sound asleep. Must be nice to be married and have children. I cannot wait to have a lot of kids, live somewhere out in the country and have cows, a horse, couple of dogs, chickens and a husband. Let me see. I am a sophomore and have two more years of high school and four years of college and will graduate when I am twenty-two. I could get married the same year and have five children by the time I am twenty-seven. That makes me think of Mindy on our basketball team. One time we were all talking about getting married and having a family and Mindy mentioned that she was going to be a coach and that she was not interested in being married and even less interested in having children. Dean saw her at one of our games and he had a hard time figuring out if she was a girl or a boy. I don't care what she is. She's really nice and the best player on our team and maybe marriage is not for everyone. God help me, I sound like Mom.

Cannot think of anything else to write about. Am going to see what's on TV and hope I don't fall asleep. I did last time and didn't even hear the Myers' get home.

❦   ❦   ❦

Sam, there was nothing in the world that Dad or I wouldn't do for you. However, I changed my thinking after you had that slumber party in sixth grade. After that night, I thought that I would do anything for you, with the exception of organizing another all-night party. I hated it and yes, I did mention something about pigs flying. Anyway, I tried to tell Emma that having five or six teenagers over might make for a long night. Emma didn't listen to me and said that, just because I had a bad experience a few years ago, did not mean that it was going to happen to her. Dad and Dean were camping that night, you were at Pam's and I was looking forward to having the whole house to myself.

Sam, when the phone rang at two o'clock in the morning, I prayed that it was an obscene phone call and not Dad, telling me that something had happened to Dean or vice versa. Oh my God, I sound just like your grandmother, but how could I? We're not even related. It was neither. It was Emma, who wanted me to be the first to know that three girls were barfing all over their sleeping bags and she asked me to come over and help her clean up the mess. I told Emma that there was a limit to friendship, but I went over anyway, after she mentioned that you were one of the barfers.

I got dressed and drove over to Emma's. She was standing in the middle of the yard with a cigarette in one hand and a garden hose in the other, hosing down sleeping bags and nightgowns. Emma thought that the pizza might have been spoiled. Truthfully, I thought that one of the girls just got sick and that the smell made the others throw up, because that's what I felt like doing when I smelled the sleeping bags. Emma thought that I might be right, but just in case I wasn't, she called the all-night pizza place and asked to speak to the manager. She talked to the manager for quite a while and then said, "Sir, you make that four and you got yourself a deal. Thank you so very much for being so understanding." So, Emma got four free pizzas a month for a year. I wrote Emma's sentence down, not because it contained any profundity, but because it was the longest sentence I had ever heard her utter without a single curse word.

CHAPTER 20

❀

(July)

This summer s going by in a hurry. Haven't written much in it lately. Am not working today and I feel like catching up on some things. I did real well in school last year and made nothing below a 95. Dean also made all A's and Mom and Dad were pretty thrilled with us. Pam's G.P.A. was 100.5. She is so smart. Cannot believe that I will be a junior when we go back and Dean will start his last year.

I have been working in the "Three in One" all summer and I love it. It's a clothes store and most of the customers are teenagers. I get four dollars an hour, which is pretty good and I average about thirty to forty hours a week, not too shabby and I also get a discount. Dad is making me put half of my paycheck in my savings account. I have to come up with a couple of thousand dollars by my senior year. Dad will match the amount and then I can buy a used car. Cannot wait.

Dean is working at the Big R Ranch, which he has done for the past few summers. He gets paid a lot more than I do and he has no trouble saving like I do. He never seems to spend any money and he hates shopping. I bought Dean a shirt at the "Three in One" last week, not the kind he usually wears, but one with big sleeves and a lot of pockets. He liked it and wore it when he went out with some girl. I feel sorry for any girl who has a date with Dean, because he never seems to date any girl more than just the one time.

Pam is working as a waitress in a restaurant. She really doesn't like it very much and she has rotten hours, but she makes a lot in tips. In spite of the fact that we are both working, we have seen a lot of each other. She met this guy in the restaurant and had a few dates with him, but then she got tired of him. As far as my dating is concerned, I am not doing real well in that department. I would like to, but I've never gone out with a boy I would like to date more than once. Hey Dean, we do have something in common! Alan and I go out once in a while, but we are just friends and we only kissed one time and both decided that we could have done without it. Once in a while a bunch of us go out for pizza or burgers and a movie and that's more fun than just going out with one person. I just re-read this paragraph and it sounds familiar. I am fairly sure that I said the same thing last year.

I got pretty mad at Mom today. I am over it now, but I still want to write it down. Don't remember the last time I got pissed at her, but I did big time this afternoon. A few weeks ago when I was on my lunch break, I met some kids at a hamburger place. Two of the girls go to my school, but I had never really talked to any of them. They were nice, but a little weird and the guys they were with had earrings and pony tails. I talked to one of the girls the next day in the mall. Anyway, to make a long story short, three of the girls and a few boys stopped by the house earlier today and asked me to go out with them for a couple of hours. Didn't have anything else to do and it sounded like fun. Mom and Dad were working in the yard and I told them I was leaving for a while. Mom took one quick look at the group, waved very friendly-like, said "How are you all today?" to them and "No way" to me. Dad shook their hands. I asked her what I was supposed to tell them and she said that it made no difference to her just as long as my answer contained "No, I cannot go." I was so pissed. I made up this excuse that sounded unbelievable, even to myself, and they left, driving like a bat out of hell. I told Mom that they were my friends and that she had no right to judge them by their looks. Told her and Dad that just because they looked different didn't mean that they were drug addicts or alcoholics and also pointed out to them that I was old enough to choose my own friends. Big, big, mistake, because Dad immediately said, "Evidently you are not, Sam."

Mom said that she realized that looks did not mean everything, but that they meant plenty to her in this case and that she would not allow me to run around with that group and, since when were they my friends? I told Mom that she could be pretty mean and she said that she was tired of this conversation and did not want to hear another word. It was, as far as she was concerned, a very trivial matter. Then I yelled at her that it wasn't a trivial matter, but a very big issue. Dad told me not to raise my voice at Mom. He also said that he was far from old fashioned, but he didn't appreciate that pony-tailed kid in the combat boots telling him "Yo man" when he met him. I thought it was totally useless to talk to them, so I went to my room.

It's several hours later now and I am completely over my mad and I don't understand myself at times. Why did I get so effin' upset? Mom was right. They're not my friends and I could understand what Dad and Mom were thinking and saying and they are probably right. I really should go downstairs and tell them that I am sorry about blowing up, but I have the hardest time doing that. Sometimes, not very often, I wish I could be more like Mom. I used to make her so very mad and she would blow up and say a lot of things. Then later, she would tell me that she regretted some of the things she had said and apologized. She said that sometimes I made her so angry and she let her temper take over.

(Later)

I went downstairs for a while and am now back in my room. I really surprised myself. I told Mom and Dad that I was sorry and, since the words came so easily, I told them twice. I just thought of something: I hardly ever write something nice or complimentary about Mom and that's not nice. She can be so overprotective and always wants to know where I am going when I go out and with whom. A long time ago, when we still argued a lot, I asked her why she could not leave me alone and she said that would be very easy to do if she did not love me so much. She and I are really getting along now and she can be a lot of fun and she makes me laugh. Another good thing about her is that she never seems embarrassed or surprised by anything I tell her.

Mom said a while ago, when I was downstairs, that getting unnecessarily upset over something is all right and that everyone loses control over her or his feelings once in a while. Then she made the mistake of adding, "even I." and Dad winked at me. I asked Mom if she was referring to the recent racquetball tournament. Mom said that she had not lost her temper at the tournament, and that it had been just a misunderstanding between her and Dad. Dad and I laughed and I asked her if she really felt that way about it and she said, "Not for a minute, Honey, but it sounds so much better than admitting that I made a horse's ass of myself."

Every time I think about that day, I have to laugh. Dad joined a health club a few months ago and the club has two racquetball courts. Dean and I played there a few times and it was fun. Dad told Mom that it would be nice to do more things together, so he changed his single membership to a family one. Mom played a few times. Said she didn't particularly care for the game, but liked the exercise and she got good real fast. Then Dad came home and announced that the club was having a tournament and that he had signed himself and Mom up in mixed doubles. Mom rolled her eyes and whispered, "Oh Brian, how could you? You must have rocks in your head." She finally agreed to it. I went to the tournament. Dean didn't want to go and he missed a helluva lot. He would have liked the free pizza, donuts and sodas. There were a lot of guys from our school playing in the singles round, and I watched them more than Mom and Dad. Anyway, it was a round robin and Mom and Dad had to play a total of four rounds. They won the first round, in spite of Dad, who is not all that great. In the next round, Dad accidentally hit the woman on the other team with his racquet and she had to sit down for a few minutes. That freaked him out and he never hit another ball, except when he had to serve, so Mom had to do all the running. In the third round, Dad was going for a shot and he knocked Mom down and fell on top of her, sweaty and all. Some men who were watching the match yelled to Dad that screwing on the court was not allowed. Dad thought it was funny, but I could tell by the look on Mom's face that she was getting pretty pissed. They played their last round at six. Quite a few people watched that match. They were probably hanging around just to see what Dad was going to do for an encore. He did not disappoint them. He hit both their opponents, knocked Mom against the wall twice and hit himself in the leg so badly that he needed a bandage. Mom completely ignored him, she was so ticked off. As soon as they got off the court, Mom said that she was ready to go home, but Dad wanted to hang around for a few minutes, and so we all did.

In the car, on the way home, Dad said that he could not remember the last time he had such a good time and he told Mom that he was anxiously waiting for the next tournament. Mom said that his smugness was very unbecoming. Think she would have worded it differently if I had not been in the back seat. Then she said that Dad had deeply embarrassed her and Dad got pissed, at least I think he was ticked off, because he raised his voice at Mom and he never does that and he called her "Helen" instead of "Honey". "I beg your pardon, Helen, but you got it mixed up. It was your childish behavior that made me feel ill at ease." Mom denied that she had acted like an imbecile. Then Dad made a mistake of cosmic proportion when he told Mom, "Helen, it just dawned on me why you are acting this way. It bothers you that it was me who received the trophy for good sportsmanship and not you." and that did it for Mom. She told Dad that she'd rather walk home than ride in the car with a person oozing with sarcasm and she asked him to stop the car and Dad did. When we drove off, Mom yelled something. Dad asked me if I understood what she was saying, and I told him that it had something to do with the trophy and his ass. Dad and I laughed all the way home.

That's the first time I have ever heard Mom and Dad argue that loudly and what a stupid thing to fight about. Talk about immature and childish behavior. Mom has a way to go in that department. All this took me forever to write down and my hand is tired. Am going to stop for the night.

*   *   *

Sam, before I comment on that blasted tournament, an event I'd rather not dwell on too long, I'd like to thank you for finally mentioning some positive things about me. I am glad you felt you could tell me anything, but you were mistaken in stating that nothing embarrassed or surprised me. Many a time, when you talked about things that were off the wall, I didn't know how to react and, consequently, I did not say much. I asked Emma one time if Pam's conversations ever made her feel uncomfortable. Emma said that she was always so damned happy when Pam talked to her, something Emma didn't think happened often enough, that it didn't matter to her what Pam talked about or how she said it. Emma said that times had changed so much and it wasn't always easy for her to relate to her daughters.

Well, I may as well bite the bullet and say a few things, as few as possible, about my behavior after that tournament. The club was about five miles from our home, and I wished that I had not gotten mad at Dad right after we got into the car, because I did not enjoy the long walk, which put me in an even worse mood. When I got home, Dad had evidently already showered and he smelled so good. He was in the kitchen, fixing hamburgers and a salad, the table was set, nice music was playing on the stereo and all my anger vanished. I looked at this handsome and exceptional man and thought how fortunate and very blessed I was to share my life with him. Then I apologized for my inconsiderate, childish, etc. etc. etc. behavior and Dad just said, no never mind what Dad said. His comment was sacred and he might not appreciate me repeating it. On second thought, I wonder if Dad remembers what he said. Sam, I just asked him and he said that he remembered every word as if he had just spoken them a few minutes ago, but he didn't repeat them, so I am pretty sure that he has no recollection. So much for sacredness.

Sam, I also remember apologizing to you for witnessing my obnoxious behavior. You patted me on the head and told me not to worry, and that everybody flares up now and then and that it was not always easy to contemplate life in a detached manner. It hit me, Sam, and I thought that you were maturing at a faster rate that I was.

CHAPTER 21

❀

(September)

I always thought that high school would get progressively more difficult but, so far, this semester has been fairly easy, even though I am taking some hard classes. I used to waste a lot of time when I got home from school, at least a couple of hours, before I would settle down to study, but I cannot do that anymore. I try to get all my work done right after I get home from basketball practice and still manage to have some time for other things.

Working in the "Three in One" was great and I am going to do it again next summer. They wanted me to continue working there on week ends, but I decided against it. Have too much to do and cannot fit it all in.

My favorite class is still English. I just love it and also the teacher. I hate economics. The only thing I like about that irritating class is that I am sitting two rows behind John Griffin, Dean's friend from the track team. Whenever I get bored in that class, which is about all the time, I look over at him and I drool. Don't think I am the only one. There seem to be quite a few droolers in that class. He is just gorgeous and I'd give anything to go out with him, but I know that my chances are slim to none.

I asked Dean about him, but I should have known better than to waste my time and breath, and energy. Dean didn't say much, except that John was one of the best runners on the team. Dean, you are a turd. Speed on the track field is not what I am interested in. I want to know about his dating habits and everything else you know about his social life. I don't want to ask anyone in school about John, because I don't want it to get around that I like him. Like him? Did I say that? "Like" is the understatement of the year. I think that I am actually madly in love with him, especially with his back, which is the only part of his body I am very familiar with and I would give my eyetooth to have a date with him. I told Pam what I thought of John. She doesn't think he's all that cool looking. I told her she had rotten taste.

Mom is downstairs, talking to a lady she met when they were both living in the dorm in their freshman year. She called yesterday and after Mom hung up the phone she said that she had no earthly idea to whom she had been talking but that, whoever it was, was coming over today. Mom got her year book out of the attic and when she found the woman's picture, she said, "Oh shit, not that Jane." I am listening a little to Mom's and Jane's conversation. Mom is using her formal voice, the one she reserves for PTA meetings and when talking to people in Dad's company, so I gather that she's not having a good time. Mom called upstairs and told me to get ready for the seven-thirty booster club meeting. Booster club meeting? We don't go to any of those meetings. I got it. She's trying to get rid of Jane. I told her I was ready to go any time she was.

(Later)

Mom and I just got home from driving around. Mom said that she hated nothing more than lying, but she saw no other way to get rid of this annoying woman, who was so consumed with her own self-importance. That reminds me. I need to tell Mom that she said "shit" yesterday and that she owes a nickel. After I tell her, she will probably owe a dollar. I need to explain what I am talking about. A few weeks ago, Dad made this wooden "curse box" in his workshop. It's really nice looking. No bigger than a shoe box. He told us that he didn't think that the language in our family was up to par and he said that we should make a serious effort to express ourselves without execrations. I asked Mom what that word means and she said, "bull crap" and then she said that since Dad and Dean hardly ever use strong language, she and I should take this box very personally. Dean told Dad that he thought it was a stupid idea, and Mom and I immediately agreed with him. I asked him how long it had taken him to make this box and he proudly said that it had taken him "only a couple of hours." Mom said that he could have mowed the yard and trimmed the bushes around the house in "only a couple of hours." Anyway. Dad wrote every word from asshole to tit face (Where did he get that last word? We've never used it.) On the box and the value of each word. Darn, shit, damn and many others are only a dime, but the mother of them all, the infamous "F" word, and anything else that starts with an F is fifty cents and whenever we use any of the words listed on the box, we have to put the appropriate amount in the box. Mom, Dean and I thought it was the dumbest thing Dad had ever come up with. Mom told Dad that she thought we were all entirely too old to participate in this childishness and Dad told her that she was also entirely too old to use unladylike language and Mom said, "Helen, when, oh when, are you ever going to learn to keep your mouth shut."

Dad hardly ever curses. The only time I have ever heard him say anything was after a policeman wrote him a ticket for not having a current safety sticker on his car and Dad called him a "friggin' ferret face". Mom did a lot better after she got a speeding ticket and had to take seven hours of defensive driving. She uses "shit" a lot, but hates the "F" word and doesn't want me or Dean, as if he would, to ever use it in her presence.

Dean had to be in school real early the other day, so Mom had to take me to school at seven-thirty. She was still half asleep and opened the wrong garage door and when she backed the car out, she rammed it against the door and the entire door was all bent to hell. Didn't do much damage, but the door needed some new panels. Anyway. Mom quietly said, "Excuse me for a minute, Honey" and then she let out a string of words that would have made a sailor blush, as Dad would say. I kept track of her curse words and told her that she owed the stupid box eight dollars and fifty cents.

Later that day, Dean asked what we were going to do when that idiot box was full. Should not take too long. She said that she didn't know yet, but that it might be a nice idea to donate it to the church. Dean suggested that we also put Dad's stupid work of art in the collection box. Mom and Dad have been going to church religiously lately and they would like nothing better than for me and Dean to go with them, but we always come up with some lame excuse why we cannot go. Mom even went one afternoon last week and I don't know why. Going once a week, on Sunday, would be plenty for me. Dean and I went to Sunday school for years when we were younger and we liked it most of the time and then we started going to church with Mom and Dad for quite a few years until the church got a new minister, a sanctimonious and pompous ass, as Mom called him. We stopped going, but now the church has a new minister and Mom and Dad seem to like him all right.

Cannot believe that I am going to be seventeen next month. Have already been driving for a year and still like it. Dean and I are sharing a car and it is working out pretty well most of the time.

❦   ❦   ❦

Jane was a real pain our freshman year. She had a blind date at the beginning of our first semester and she fell head-over-heels in love with him. After this date, whenever she had to step out for a few minutes, she would knock on everyone's door and tell us to please tell Ron, that she would be back momentarily. He never called her, but that did not discourage her and she kept bugging us the entire year. The only thing I enjoyed about Jane's visit was the fact that she had not aged nearly as well as I had. Who knows, she probably told her husband that she looked a lot better than I did.

Sam, it was sweet of you to tell me how much I owed the box after I hit the garage door, but, in reality, I didn't owe a single cent. Dad had neglected to tell us, but I knew it was implied, that curse words voiced under extraneous circumstances do not count. Also, even if the conditions had not been relevant, I would have received a hundred per cent discount, simply because the accident took place between the hours of seven and eight in the morning, I was wearing blue and the sky was very cloudy.

When Emma came over and saw the box, she told Dad that she thought the world of him but that this box was ridiculous. Then she said, "Time me, Brian. I bet you anything that I can fill up this little mother in less than ten minutes." Dad could not stop laughing. I always loved to see and hear Dad laugh. He would throw his head back and his laugh was deep and infectious.

Yes, Sam, I did go to church one afternoon, but my visit had nothing whatsoever to do with a sudden desire to pray in a quiet place. Some friends and I had gone out for lunch and on the way home I started regretting the several spicy tacos I had consumed and I needed a bathroom and I needed it right then. I passed a library, but it was closed and I had no alternative but to go to this church which was adjacent to the library. It did not seem right to just run in, use the facilities and run out, so I sat down in one of the pews and did some meditating and I also thanked God for giving some of His flock the insight to build that church right there. All in all, I sat there for at least half an hour, a very relieving and also extremely peaceful thirty minutes. Sam, Dad and I were often very sorry that you and Dean were not all that interested in going to church. We didn't think that we could make you go; all we could do was encourage you. We tried to get Emma to come to church with us, but she declined. She said that as soon as they allowed smoking in church, she'd take us up on our offer. Her idea of worshiping was to fix herself a big pot of coffee on

Sunday morning, turn the radio to a local station that broadcasted a service, light a cigarette, listen to the sermon in her nightgown and say, "Amen, that was very inspiring." when it was over.

CHAPTER 22

❀

(November)

It's Friday afternoon and I am so happy that the week is over and that we have no school for two whole days. Next week is going to be short, just Monday through Wednesday and then we have four days off for Thanksgiving. I cannot wait. Grandma and Grandpa are flying in Wednesday evening, just for two nights. We haven't seen them since last year. Grandma called this morning and told Mom that she was feeling "poorly". I asked Mom how "poorly" she was, and Mom said undoubtedly not enough to cancel the flight.

Pam is spending Thanksgiving night with us. She and I are going to get up early on Friday, drive to Houston and spend as many hours as possible in the Galleria and then drive home. I cannot believe that our mothers are finally letting us do something like that. However, we have to call them when we get there, and then again just before we leave. I asked Pam what she thought of that and Pam said that a phone call only took a second, so she didn't care. Sometimes I feel that Pam is so much older than I am instead of just a few months. She is just a whole lot more you-know-what (mature) than I am.

We are really looking forward to the trip. I need to make some money between now and then because I am flat broke and I would like to have at least a hundred dollars. Mom said that she'll pay me to clean the house this weekend and Dad said I can wash his car. Don't think that's going to add up to the amount I have in mind. Maybe I can entertain Grandma over the holidays to keep her out of Mom's hair. Think Mom would pay me at least ten an hour to do that. Maybe I can get an advance on my allowance, but I don't think so, since I believe I have been advanced well into the month of January.

I turned seventeen last month. Some friends and Pam had a surprise party for me at Macie's house. Pam and I talked about surprise parties a long time ago and we both decided that we did not ever want to be surprised. We also said that if one was ever organized for either one of us, we'd mention it. I think that Pam conveniently forgot all about this conversation. When I bitched about it later she said that, since the conversation took place such a long time ago, she was afraid that I might have changed my mind and she did not want to be the one to ruin the surprise. It really was a fun evening, though, and it was so sweet of Macie and Pam to get it together.

O.K. What was I talking about earlier? Oh yes, going to Houston. After what happened earlier this week, I am surprised that we can still go to Houston next Friday. A couple of weeks ago, Pam and I were talking about the fact that we really never do anything we're not supposed to do, like skipping school or something, and the moment we mentioned that, we decided to do it. Neither one of us has a car, so we asked Anne, who owns a piece of barely drivable shit, to come with us. Anne said that she skipped all the time and that it was a piece of cake. We decided to take Tuesday off. As soon as Dean and I got to school, I waited for him to go into the building and then I walked to the back of the parking lot where Anne was supposed to pick me and Pam up. Pam was already there, but Anne was nowhere to be found. We were afraid that she had chickened out and that would have been bad because we didn't feel that we could go to class, since we had not done our homework. We didn't have to worry about it, because Anne did show up.

We all decided to go to the mall on the other side of town, go window shopping for a couple of hours, have lunch, and get back to school by three. We had it all figured out. Pam and I only had our lunch money and a few extra dollars, but Anne said we could borrow from her, since she had plenty. She's so lucky. Anne's car made all sorts of funny noises, but she told us not to pay any attention to it. She said it was a piece of inferior crap and it always made strange sounds. We stopped for a Coke and Pam told Anne that her tire looked a little low, and Anne said, "Oh, holy shit, I do believe we have a flat tire." Pam said that changing a tire could not be all that difficult, but it was. At first we couldn't find the jack, but we finally found it under the spare tire and we all decided that it was a stupid place to hide that important object. None of us could put the thing together. We waited for a few minutes and then this truck drove up and we asked the driver if he could help us out. He was real nice and had it done in no time at all. Pam said, "See. I was right. There's nothing to changing a tire."

When we got to the mall, it was still closed, which was a bummer. We walked around until the stores opened, looked in a lot of shops for a couple of hours and pretended to have a good time. We had lunch in a cafeteria. Pam and I didn't get a lot, because we didn't have much money and when we asked Anne if could borrow some, she said that she had spent it all. She really can be a real piss ant. After lunch we still had a few hours to kill. Pam and I got bored and we just farted around, but Anne was having a great time with one of her mother's credit cards. Pam told me that she didn't think that Anne's mother was endowed with a lot of valuable substance between her ears and I agreed.

Going to the mall is not all that relaxing or any fun if you constantly have to look over your shoulder out of fear that someone you know will see you. Also, going to the mall is pretty boring when you have no money to spend. Don't know about Anne, but Pam and I did not have a great time. Besides, we were behind on our homework and had to work our butts off that evening. Well, I had to. Pam doesn't have to study much. Pam and I were a little worried about writing an absence note to school and we had a hard time coming up with something believable. We finally decided that Pam had not been feeling well and I had been out for personal reasons. Mom's handwriting sucks and I had a hard time writing the note and making it look like she had written it, but her signature was easy, since it is illegible.

Anyway, on Wednesday, Pam and I saw Anne at her locker and she was in tears. That bird brain had left one of her mother's credit cards in the last store we were in and the sales lady called her mother. So what did Anne's mother do? She went to the principal and that nerd called Anne into his office and gave her a long lecture on responsibilities and all that crap. Anne said that her mother had grounded her indefinitely, which seemed pretty exaggerated to Pam and me. Pam and I were hoping that Anne had not mentioned either one of our names to that dick of a principal.

When Dean and I got home from school on Wednesday, Mom asked how our day had been. When I said that it was just like any other day, she asked me how my day had been yesterday, with the emphasis on yesterday. I figured that she knew that I had skipped and I did not see any point in denying it, so I told her that I skipped school yesterday. I told her to let me have it and ground me, but please, spare me one of your tedious speeches. Wonders never cease. Mom was not mad at all. She just said that if I ever had the urge to do it again, to please let her know and, of course, she had to add, "Guess how I would have felt, Honey, if I had gotten a call from the highway patrol, informing me with deep regret that my daughter had been involved in an accident. I would tell him that he was mistaken, because my sweet and innocent daughter was in school getting an education." I asked Mom how she knew I had skipped and she said, "I am your mother"and she acted like that was a perfectly logical explanation. I also asked Mom why she was not mad. She said that I was a good daughter and an excellent student and if skipping school was the worst thing I had ever done, she had nothing to worry about. Mom can be pretty cool.

Pam just called and asked me to go to the movies. It's eight-thirty, and neither Pam nor I has been asked out on a date, so it is safe to assume that tonight is not our lucky evening. Pam's mother is treating us.

✹   ✹   ✹

"Being your mother" had nothing to do with it. Emma called me Wednesday morning and asked me if you had gone to school the previous day. Told her that, as far as I knew, you had. She said that she was cleaning house and found a lot of crumbled up notes in the trash can. All the notes started out with "To Whom It May Concern" in what looked like her handwriting. Emma said she thought that "our little shits" had probably skipped school. Neither Emma nor I thought that it was a big deal and we were just hoping that you had enjoyed the day. However, we thought that if we let you and Pam off the hook, you might think that we could easily be deceived and we didn't like that thought. We felt that it was our motherly duty to go to school and find out for sure, but neither one of us wanted to go. Emma said that she had not shaved her legs in days and was not going to do it for the principal, who, she thought, was a real prick and I told Emma that I had not showered yet. Also told Emma that we didn't have to talk to the prick, but just to someone in the attendance office. Emma pretended not to hear me. She said she was going to toss a coin, and, after five minutes came back to the phone and told me that I had lost, which did not surprise me. When I asked her what had taken so long, she said that the coin had rolled under the sofa. Sure, Emma.

When I walked into the attendance office, I realized that I was totally unprepared and I must have sounded like an idiot when I told the clerk that I thought my daughter might have been absent the previous day and that I could not remember if I had written an excuse or not and I asked her if she would be so kind and check the file. She came up with your note, Sam. You did an excellent job copying my handwriting. I told the sneering clerk, "That's my note all right. Now I remember writing it. Thank you so much." I am sure she told everyone in her office that Sam and Dean Evers' mother was already suffering from the onset of amnesia. I don't know why I went through all that trouble. It would have been simpler to just ask you.

Sam, you never had much idea about the value of money. Babysitting Grandma for ten dollars an hour sounded cheap to me. I would have gone as high as twenty. Thanks to doing chores and thanks to Grandpa, you had accumulated enough to go shopping in Houston. I remember that Grandma gave you and Pam a lecture on comparative shopping before you left. Later on you told me that you always considered my speeches rather boring and lengthy, but that you never realized how short and amusing they were until you had to listen to Grandma's soliloquy.

CHAPTER 23

❀

(December)

Today is the 29th. Just a few more days before we go back to school. Christmas was great, but we didn't go to Colorado this year, for the simple reason that we could not afford it. Mom and Dad were sorry and told us that we might be able to go next year.

Anne and some other girls are coming over tonight. We are going to eat here at home and then watch some movies. Mom offered to cook us a nice meal, but we're going to do it ourselves. I would rather have gone out, but I don't have any money and neither do any of my friends. I am always flat broke after Christmas. Of course, I invited Pam first, but she couldn't come because she has a date tonight with none other than my brother.

Last month, right after Thanksgiving, Dean came to my room, which he doesn't do very often, so I knew he had something on his mind. He listened to my rock music, which he hates, so I thought that was another indication that something was bothering him. Then he started talking about school and sports and he said that he and some of his friends think that I am one of the best players on the basketball team and that's when I became suspicious, because Dean is not real big on compliments. The last time he said something nice to me was Christmas morning, when he gave me a hug after he opened my present and he called me a sweet little turd.

Anyway, I had never seen Dean so talkative and I finally asked him what he really wanted. He said, "Nothing really, but do you know by any chance if Pam is going out with anyone in particular?" For God's sake. Pam and I have been friends since first grade and there's not a whole lot we don't know about each other. She'd be the first to know if I were dating and the other way around.

Boys can be dense, even when they're book smart, like Dean. Well, I told Dean that Pam was dating about as often as I was, which was zilch. I said that, since I had been a good sister and confided in him the embarrassing truth that Pam's and my social life was almost non-existent, it was only right for him to share a little information with me. He wanted to know how much "a little" was. I thought very quickly and then casually mentioned that it was a minute amount and that I was only slightly curious about when he was going to call Pam, when they were going out (assuming she accepted his date, but I knew she would), where he was taking her, what time they were going to get back, and, this was very important, was he going to ask her out more than once. He has this horrible habit of dating a girl only one time and I didn't want him to do that to Pam. Dean did not answer any of my questions and that did not surprise me. He only said that I was too nosy for his liking and that I was beginning to sound more and more like Mom every day. Me? Sound like Mom? I did ask again when they thought they might go out, and Dean said that I would know, because he wants me to iron his shirt. What am I, hi personal servant?

I was thinking that it was hard to believe that Dean was actually going to call my best friend and ask her out. Don't know if she even likes him all that much. We hardly ever talk about him. Pam teases him and treats him like a brother. I sure hope that it all works out. It's about time that Dean starts showing an interest in girls and starts dating. Shit, Dean is right. I do sound like Mom.

I was proud of myself for not telling Pam that Dean might give her a call. Don't really know what she thinks of him, but, in case she really likes him, I didn't want her to get her hopes up. It's really cool, though. Pam told me a few days later that Dean had asked her out and she sounded pretty happy and excited. They went to a movie. That night, when Dean was in the shower and getting ready, I ironed his shirt and jeans, and I even polished his boots. He looked so good and he smelled even better and he even thanked me for doing all those things for him. The few times he had a date, it would take him ten seconds to get ready and there was no ironing or boot polishing involved, so, I figured that this was an entirely different date. I couldn't wait for him to get home and ask him about his evening, but Mom and Dad told me not to bother him. I was wondering if Dean would kiss her. I bet you anything Dean is the worst and lousiest kisser on the planet. Anyway, I fell asleep before Dean got home and couldn't bug him until the next morning. However, when I saw Dean, he didn't say anything. Now, wasn't that unkind and cruel? It didn't matter that he didn't tell me anything, because Pam called right after Dean went to work at the ranch. She sounded real happy about the evening. She said that Dean even held the car door open for her. My brother, a gentleman? And yes, she volunteered the information that he gave her a quick kiss. Pam said that although she was pretty inexperienced in that department, she was pretty sure that it was not the best kiss ever. See, I knew it. I just knew that Dean would be a shitty kisser. I asked Pam if they were going out again, and she said that she would like nothing better. I am so happy for Pam and yes, also for Dean.

Pam and Dean usually go out either Friday or Saturday night and he calls her quite a lot. I asked Dean how much he really liked her and he told me to stop sounding like a four-year old, but then he smiled and said that she was great. Pam, who is usually pretty quiet, is beginning to talk a lot more and I think, by what she has told me, that she is crazy about Dean.

I asked Mom how she felt about Dean and Pam dating steadily and I had a few more questions for her. Mom said that she found the subject of genetics most interesting and it was fascinating how certain traits would skip one generation and then emerge in the next. I asked her if she minded explaining herself and Mom said, "Well, since you insist. You sound like your grandmother." Sounding like Mom is one thing, sounding like Grandma is pathetic.

I had better stop writing and get my room looking half-way decent before Anne and the others come over. Besides, I am beginning to bore myself to death.

❦   ❦   ❦

Sam, you were far from boring. Your writing was entertaining and amusing and, sometimes, very touching. You also had the enviable trait of organizing your thoughts so well on paper.

It never surprised me or Dad in the least when Dean and Pam started dating. Think he had liked her for years before he finally got up enough courage to ask her out. Emma told me that right after Pam started dating Dean, he arrived a little too early one time and Pam wasn't quite ready. Emma took that opportunity to tell Dean in no uncertain terms what she expected of him and all Dean could get in was, "Yes m'am" and "No m'am. Think that Emma scared him a little with her no-nonsense attitude and her frankness, and Dean never showed up early again. Dean was so courteous and considerate when it came to Pam. Not only did he open doors for her, he also pulled back her chair at dinner time. Dad and I always thought the world of Pam and we were so happy when Dean finally saw the light and started going out with her. Pam was so pretty and Dean so handsome and they made such a good looking couple.

Honey, how could you possibly have expected their first kiss to be perfect. First kisses never are and it makes you wonder why you are going to try it again and again anyway. The first time Dad and I kissed, we knew shit from wild honey, but it is absolutely amazing how quickly we both caught on.

CHAPTER 24

❀

(March)

Today is our last day of spring break. I had a great week and am not quite ready to go back. I checked the school calendar and it looks like we have no more days off between now and the end of May. I cannot believe that I only have one more year of high school after this year is over. Pam and I were talking abut where we want to go to college. Guess it all depends a little on our scholarships, which we hope to get. Neither one of us want to go to The University of Texas right here in town. We know that it is one of the better ones, but we want to move away from home. Not too far, mind you, just a couple of hundred miles or so. Asked Mom if she wold be disappointed if I didn't go to U.T. and she said that she never expected me to go to that university. She said that she didn't get off the banana boat yesterday and that she understood perfectly that I wanted to move away from Austin. I don't even know yet what I want to major in. Pam is so smart and can major in just about anything. I haven't been able to think of any field I might be interested enough in to spend four years of my life studying for. After reading that last sentence, it might be a good idea not to major in English.

Dean is graduating this year. It will be so strange without him and I am going to miss him. Dean is taking Pam to the junior-senior prom in May. They're still dating a lot. Dean has been so much nicer since he started dating Pam and he even talks a lot more, and so does Pam. Mom said that they're very good for each other and she is right, for once. Alan has asked me to go to the prom and I am glad. I know him pretty well and we and some other friends have been hanging out a lot and we don't bore each other to death and he's funny and we laugh a lot. We're just friends, though. Pretty soon Mom and I and Pam and her mother are going shopping for a prom dress. I told Mom that it seemed like a waste of money to me since I am only going to wear it once and Mom said, "How considerate of you. Why don't we make your dress and Pam's ourselves?" Not funny, Mom.

Spring break was the best. Pam and I and some girls wanted to drive to the coast and spend a few nights at someone's beach house, just hang around and have a blast. Mom and Dad were barely willing to discuss it and when I made the humongous mistake of telling them accidentally that there would be no supervision, they asked me to drop the subject and not to mention it again until I was twenty-one. Just when I was getting ready to tell Mom that I am seventeen and no baby anymore, she had the gall to say, "And there's absolutely no point in bringing up the fact that you're seventeen and no longer a baby." I really hate it when she does that. Pam's mother told her that she was deeply disappointed in her and she wasn't even willing to talk about it. Then Pam's dad came to town for three days and he took Pam and her sisters to Houston. Think that Dean was pretty upset about Pam being gone for a few days. He and Dad went to Lake Travis for two nights. Think they rented a boat and went fishing. Cannot think of anything more boring than fishing.

Since Dad and Dean were going to be gone for a few days and since Mom and I had no desire to go with them, not even if they had asked us, Mom suggested that we go shopping in Nuevo Laredo. When we told Dad about this trip, he wasn't too thrilled. He didn't want the two of us driving to Mexico by ourselves and he wished we would go somewhere else. He drove us crazy with all his advice and told us that we should leave the car in Laredo and, under no circumstances, should we drive into Nuevo Laredo. Mom said, "Brian, my Sweet, please give me and your daughter some credit. Of course we would never ever even dream of crossing the border in the car." Dad told me to stay with Mom at all times and when I told him that I was certainly old enough to do a little shopping by myself, he said, "I know you are, Honey, but I am not sure about Mom."

Dad and Dean left early Friday morning and Mom and I left the next day. I drove most of the way and I loved every minute of it. I must be a pretty good driver, because Mom dozed several times. We listened to tapes, talked and laughed a lot and had a ball. Dad had given us a map and he had marked the way we should go. Mom and I thought that was totally unnecessary, since there is only one highway and all you have to do is follow it, but we didn't say anything. After I had been driving for about an hour, Mom got the map out, studied it very carefully, although she doesn't know east from west and said that it seemed to her that there was a shorter way, which would save us at least an hour, so we decided to go for it. After about an hour or so, it was pretty obvious that neither one of us knew where the hell we were, but Mom still insisted that we were doing just fine. We stopped for gas and while I was filling up the tank, Mom went inside with the map to find out just how fine we were doing. Turned out that we weren't even close to where we thought we were, and we had to drive all the way back to the place where Mom thought she knew it all better and we had to start all over.

We finally got to Laredo and we checked into a zero star hotel, as Mom called it and then we drove to the border to find a parking lot, which was not the easiest thing to do. We finally found a place that we thought looked like a parking lot. Some guy came running up to us and yelled, "tenty dollar." Mom and I didn't know if the parking cost "tenty dollar" or if he was offering us that amount for our shitty car. Since Dad would not let us take Mom's car, we took mine and Dean's. Anyway, Mom gave him a twenty dollar bill, which she thought was ludicrous and we didn't even know for sure if he was the parking attendant. However, we knew for sure that he was not when he drove off like a bat out of hell in a vehicle that I wouldn't mind driving, right after we parked.

We walked across this long bridge into Nuevo Laredo. There were a lot of people hanging around the bridge. Most of the guys were pretty good-looking, but they wouldn't move an inch when we were trying to pass. Some of them talked to us, but I did not understand a word of it, even though I took Spanish for two semesters. I asked Mom how her Spanish was and she said that it wasn't very good, but she had a pretty good idea of what they might be saying. Then she said, "Sam, I am afraid to look down. Tell me the truth and do not keep anything from me to spare my feelings and my dignity. Am I wearing clothes?" I told her that she was wearing jeans, a shirt, sneakers and, hopefully, panties and a bra. She said, "Sam, you don't know what a great relief it is to hear that. I don't know about you, but the way some of these young men are looking us up and down and their snickering makes me feel that I am stark naked." We could not stop laughing.

Due to Mom's wonderful short-cuts, we did not have time to do a lot of shopping that evening. There were hundreds of little shops, but we didn't buy much. All I bought was some make up. It was a brand name and a lot cheaper than at home. Mom bought a bottle of Kahlua for Emma.

We had a sandwich for dinner and then we went up to the room and Mom took a shower. I experimented with the new make up and asked Mom how she liked the result. She said that she did not think it was possible that she was in the same room with Tammy Faye Baker and then she had to explain who that was. We watched "Dirty Dancing" on TV. Had already seen it three times and once even on the stage, but I still like it. I asked Mom what Kahlua tasted like and she said that she had no idea, but that Emma would probably let us taste it, but I told her what a bonding experience it would be to have my first real drink with my mother. That did it and she opened the bottle and we poured a little in two paper cups we found in the bathroom. We both liked it. Mom said that anything that tasted that good could not possibly contain any alcohol, so we had a little more.

The next morning, we checked out of the hotel, packed the trunk and had breakfast. Then we drove to the border, ready to do some very serious shopping. The lot where we had parked the car the day before was full. We drove around for the longest time, trying to find a place within walking distance, but we were unsuccessful. Mom was driving and that was a big, no, a huge mistake, because before we knew it, she was in the wrong lane and we ended up in front of the toll booth. There was no way she could make a U-turn, and she told the guy at the booth that she was very sorry about making a mistake, but that she had no inclination or desire to drive across the border and what could she do. The man was not friendly at all, just very sarcastic and he said, "What do you want me to do, lady? Look behind you. See all those thousands of cars? Do you want me to tell them to back up so that you can get out?" Mom can be pretty sarcastic herself and she said, "That would be most appreciated. How very considerate of you." When we asked him about driving back, he said, "Same bridge, isn't it?" I told mom that he was a genuine asshole and Mom said that I was too complimentary.

We drove into Nuevo Laredo. Had a hard time finding a parking place, but we did. It was right in front of a church. We shopped for hours and I bought a lot of things, mainly silver jewelry and some T-shirts and Mom bought a whole lot of different nativity scenes for Christmas presents and a bottle of Kahlua for Pam's mother. I told her that it seemed too early to think about Christmas, but she didn't think so. Said she was late this year, since she usually starts shopping for Christmas presents in January when everything is on sale. Mom bought me a blue leather skirt. It looks so cool and I cannot wait to wear it to school tomorrow. We also went to some stores that sold beautiful art work, but we didn't buy anything. And we walked around Nuevo Laredo and enjoyed seeing some of their churches and old buildings and then we had the best meal in a tiny restaurant with the friendliest people. It was fun. All the people were so nice.

There was a lot of traffic in Nuevo Laredo and the drive to the place where you cross the border again, took almost two hours. Some cars were waved through, but others had to wait in line and our car was one of the others. This huge lady in uniform came up to our car. She asked us to get out and we had to show her our insurance papers, registration papers, etc. She wanted to know what we had bought and we told her that all our purchases were on the back-seat. Then she made us open the trunk and she went through everything, even our dirty clothes. I sure would not want that job. She never said a word and she looked pretty mad, but boy, did she smile when she found the open Kahlua. That bottle started the longest argument in history, so I am going to give the abridged version. It finally got down to that woman telling Mom, "M'am, you just got through telling me that you only have one bottle, but that was a lie, wasn't it? You are hiding one in the trunk and I am sure you know that bring-ing in more than one bottle is illegal." Mom is pretty honest and she doesn't like lying and I could tell that she was getting pretty pissed with the drift of the conversation, but she controlled herself and quietly explained the situation. We had to follow that woman to her supervisor and had to go through the whole discussion again. Mom finally told him that this whole situation was getting ridiculous and asked him to just tell her what to do with the friggin' (she didn't really say that, but she wanted to) bottle, so that we could be on our way. He said that we could cross the border again and exchange it for two six-packs of beer. Mom looked at him for a long time and then said, "Well, that is a very tempting suggestion, but we are pressed for time. What other alternative do we have?" He said that we could leave the bottle with him and Mom said that seemed like a sensible solution to this very minor problem. Mom walked back to the car, got the bottle of Kahlua, emptied it in the drain next to the car, gave him the empty bottle and said very sweetly that she was sorry for the inconve-nience and she hoped that she had not taken up too much of his valuable time. Then she drove away as fast as our car could go, and that wasn't real speedy. I asked Mom if she had felt scared, and she said that she hadn't. Said she cannot think of being afraid when she's irate. Irate, Mom? "Yes, Honey, I was totally pissed off."

I drove most of the way back. Just before we got to Austin, I asked Mom if she was going to tell Dad about the incident at the border. Se said, "Honey, Dad and I have been happily married for almost two decades. We have always been open and honest with each other, and I feel that there's nothing I cannot discuss with him and, hell no, I am not going to mention this to him." I asked Mom if I could tell Dean and Dad about getting lost on the way to Laredo. She thought that it might be a real good idea to tell Dad very little, if anything, about this trip.

Well. It was a great spring break. I wouldn't mind going back to Nuevo Laredo again. Would be fun to go with Pam one of these days.

❧   ❧   ❧

Sam, didn't we have the best time in Laredo and didn't we laugh a lot? Think that's one of the few times we went away together and I wish that we had done it more often. When I gave Emma the bottle of Kahlua and told her about all the trouble we had gone through at the border, she said that she would treasure this gift for a long time before opening it, and then she would only consume a little of it at the time to make it last until our next visit to Laredo. Well, about a week later, Dad had to go out of town, and I went over to Emma's and told her how nice it would be to have a sip of that delicious liquor. Emma's comment was, "Helen, it's time to go back to Laredo."

CHAPTER 25

❁

(April)

It's Friday evening, usually my favorite night of the week, but not this time. I am kinda irritated. I usually have something planned for either Friday or Saturday night and I start looking forward to that at the beginning of the week. This week-end, however, is going to be a crappy one. I was invited to spend tonight and all day tomorrow at Susan's grandparent's lake house. No, I cannot go, because tomorrow morning we have to leave real early for Kerrville where I have to accept a ribbon for an English assignment and I have to attend a workshop. I could care less about going and even less about the damned ribbon. Mom wrote the poem, so let her go to Kerrville and have a boring day.

A couple of weeks ago, we had an out-of-town basketball game on a weeknight. We got home late and I still had a shit load of homework and study for two tests. At eleven, I still had to start studying for one of them and I also had to write a stupid poem for English. English is still my favorite class, but we had been studying poems for three weeks and I was getting sick of them all. Mom asked me if she could help me and I asked her to please write that poem and I gave her all the guide lines. Mom said that having guide lines for a poem didn't make a whole lot of sense, because wasn't it supposed to be from the heart? Told Mom I had no time to discuss it. Well, she did it, it sounded fairly good and it took me only a few minutes to type it. So, it comes down to the fact that if Mom had spent a little less effort on that English assignment, I might now be on my way to the lake and have a terrific time.

Mom cannot go tomorrow, which is pretty lucky for her, because I would probably drive her up the wall with all my bitching. She has to clean house and do grocery shopping, because Uncle Hank, her brother, and his family are coming for a visit. Dad is taking me and we're giving Curtis a ride. He won a ribbon for a history assignment and he is about as thrilled about going as I am. He's taking us out for lunch, drop us off at the high school, stay a few minutes for the damned presentation and then he'll pick us up later. A few minutes ago I went downstairs to ask him if he was going to the workshop with me. He was in the garage getting his fishing gear together, so I knew what the answer was going to be and I didn't bother to ask him.

I am going to feel very embarrassed accepting a ribbon for something I cannot take credit for. Mom and Dad don't believe in doing my homework for me, unless it is absolutely necessary, and I wish that Mom had stuck to that. She helped Dean out one time when he was a freshman or sophomore, I cannot remember. He had to do a wildflower collection for biology. Mom saw him walking along the road with a little bouquet of pink and white flowers which were wilted and past the point of being able to be identified. Mom felt sorry for him and she did the whole project that week-end. She did it twice and we kept one for me to hand in the following year when I took biology, which, by the way, I hated with a passion. Whatever. Riding to Kerrville with Dad and Curtis may not be all that bad. Curtis is a lot of fun. I wonder if he did his own project or if his parents helped him with it. Don't think I am going to ask him. Mom said it is a very delicate subject and the less said, the better.

Macie just called a few minutes ago and invited me to a surprise birthday party for one of her friends tomorrow evening. I asked Mom if I could go and she said "No". She's not in the best of moods, because she has to clean house and do grocery shopping, which she hates to do. She said that we haven't seen Uncle Hank, his wife and their two daughters in years and she would like for me to stay home tomorrow evening and entertain my cousins. They also have to sleep in my room for two nights and I am not too thrilled about that, because it means that I have to straighten up my mess.

I am tired of writing. In a little while I'm going to Pam's and watch a movie with her. Dean had to work tonight. Tomorrow evening he wanted to take Pam out to eat and then go to a movie. Mom wasn't too happy about that. She told Dean that we never get to see her brother and that it would be nice if Dean had dinner with us. He didn't think that was nice at all. Mom said that she didn't care what he thought, just as long as she saw his body at the dinner table and a smile on his face. She suggested that he invite Pam for dinner and then they could do whatever they wanted to afterwards. Then she regretted her last statement and spent half an hour explaining what she meant by saying "whatever they wanted to do afterwards."

In a way I am looking forward to seeing Uncle Hank. I asked Mom when we saw him last and she thinks it must have been about four years ago. He works for a pharmaceutical company in Canada. I promised Mom I would run the vacuum cleaner for her. Think I'll do that real quick before I go to Pam's. Don't know why Mom makes such a big deal out of it. I only sweep where we walk and I refuse to move any furniture, so it doesn't take me all that long.

(One week later)

I hate to admit it, but last week-end was the best. First, Dad took me and Curtis to Kerrville. He let us play any tape we wanted and we educated him about our favorite rock bands. Curtis and I asked him what he thought about it and Dad said that he was not prejudiced and hated all the groups equally. The workshop was very boring and I put the ribbon in the bottom of one of my drawers.

Mom and Dad picked up Hank and his family at the airport on Saturday. He's married to Mona and she is not a lot of fun. Grace is their oldest daughter and she is Dean's age and a senior in high school and the other daughter's name is Monica and she's fourteen. Grace is funny. Monica doesn't have a whole lot to say. Mona is all right, but she as the personality of a crouton and I don't know if I like her all that much. She treats her kids like they're still babies. She's also so damned lazy. Just sits on the sofa and orders Hank around. Dad and Hank get along well, but Dad doesn't seem to have a whole lot to talk about with Mona. Truthfully, Mom doesn't either, but she tries to be nice to her. Am glad that Dean and I don't have to call them aunt and uncle. Hank is really cool. He calls Mom "Missy" and they really like each other. They also look alike, except Hank is a lot better looking. He helped Mom in the kitchen and they talked and laughed a lot. Dad got stuck with Mona and I don't think he was too happy about it. Mom told him later that payback was a bitch and if she could put up with his parents every single Thanksgiving, the least he could do was tolerate Mona once very four years or so..

Mom fixed dinner and it was good. It was something that her mother used to make and it was Hank's favorite. Hank told her that it tasted even better than when their mother had prepared it and, if I didn't know Mom better, I could have sworn that her eyes filled with tears when he said that. Dinner couldn't be over soon enough for Dean, who was itching to take Pam out and they left about thirty-one seconds after we had dessert. By the time Grace, Monica and I finished straightening up the kitchen it was almost nine o'clock. Grace looked at the paper and wanted to go see a movie and I didn't mind at all. Mom said that was just fine with her, but Mona had to butt in and say that it was getting late. Grace said, "Well, so what?" If I had used that tone of voice to Mom, she would have said that a movie was out of the question, but Mona didn't say anything. She finally agreed that it would be O.K. for us to go, on one condition; it had to be a P.G. movie, because Monica was not old enough to see an R-rated one. Grace said that she knew that and the thought of exposing her sister to an R-rated movie would never enter her mind. As soon as we got in the car, Grace said, "To hell with P.G. We're going to see something really R and Monica, if there's any screwing, just close your eyes." We went to see "Fatal Attraction", which was definitely R. Grace and I were so engrossed in the movie and we never paid any attention to Monica. Bet she didn't close her eyes. Bet she didn't even blink. Grace said that she and Monica had to lie once in a while, because if they didn't, they would never get to do anything that kids their age enjoy. I felt sorry for both of them. After the movie we stopped for a coke and we got home pretty late.

Mom, Dad and Hank were still up and Mona was just about ready to go to bed. She asked us what we had seen and Grace told her that it was just a stupid P.G. movie, but that Monica had liked it. Cannot believe the way she lies and gets away with it. Mom would mention that she had never been a passenger in a turnip truck and she would see through all that shit immediately. Grace is a lot of fun, but Monica is so damned quiet and acts like a scared mouse. We had put two mattresses on the floor in my room for them to sleep on. Monica fell asleep immediately, well, she probably pretended to be asleep. Grace and I talked for hours, well, she did most of the talking and I did all the listening. Grace asked me if I had ever done "it". I was sure that she was talking about the same "it" that I was thinking of, but still, I could not believe her asking that. Even Pam and I never talk about sex very much. Well, I had to tell her that I had never done it and that I didn't even know anybody well enough to do it with and that, even if I did, I might not do it for a long time. Grace said that she has done it several times with her boyfriend. She said that one time she didn't get her period for six weeks and she was afraid she might be pregnant and she panicked. She didn't dare tell her mother and I didn't blame her. She told Hank and he made an appointment with a doctor for her and it turned out that she wasn't. I asked her if the doctor put her on birth control pills and he did. Grace is only Dean's age, but she acts so much older. I really like her, but all that talk about sex made me feel a little uncomfortable and also very young. All in all, it was a very educational evening.

Grace said that her parents want her to get a college education, but she has no intention of studying for another four years, just to please her folks. Her grades are evidently not all that great and she wouldn't know what to major in since she's totally disinterested. I am not going to Mom about this, because she might say that Screwing 101 might be a good basic course to get her a little enthusiastic about higher education. All Grace wants to do is get out of high school, find a job and work until she meets a man, marry him and raise a family. Grace sounds so hard and I feel sorry for her.

I got up early the next morning and Mom was already in the kitchen fixing a big breakfast. She asked me how I had liked "Fatal Attraction" and what I thought of the sex scenes in the elevator and in the kitchen sink. How did she know that we saw that movie? Anyway, we talked for a while and I told Mom that I thought that the elevator was all right, but making love in a kitchen sink filled with dirty dishes did not look all that comfortable to me. Mom said that it had nothing to do with making love, but with lust. I told Mom that a long time ago I thought that parents did not sleep together, well, I mean did not have sex, all that often and that she and Dad had only done it twice? I made that whole sentence like a question in hopes that she might do some explaining, but she said, "Sam, before I can answer your badly worded half-ass question, you have to be a little more explicit. What exactly do you mean. Twice an hour? Twice a night? Twice a day? Twice a year?" Then Dad walked in and I told her to forget it and Mom hugged him and called him her savior.

Dad and Hank left after breakfast. No idea where they went, but they were gone for several hours. Mona did not get up until noon and by that time the leftover scrambled eggs, bacon and whatever else Mom had fixed looked pretty pitiful and Mona didn't want any of it. Mom offered to fix her something, but she refused. Felt a little sorry for Mom. She's trying to be civil to Mona because she's married to her brother, but Mona doesn't appreciate anything. I picked Pam up and we showed Monica and Grace all around town and then went to the mall for a while, where Grace charged two outfits to Mona's credit cards. I wonder if Mom would let me have a card. Not worth bringing up that subject. She'd probably say that, of course, I could have my own card, I could have a dozen of them, just as long as I pay the bills at the end of the month.

Dad took us all out for dinner Sunday evening. Went to bed pretty early that night. Hank and his family left early on Monday. It really was a good week-end.

❦　　　❦　　　❦

Sam, I deeply regretted having done your English homework for you. How could you say that my poem sounded "fairly good". Emma, as nosy as all get out, saw the crumpled up paper with my efforts on it the next day, straightened it out, read it and she said that Elizabeth Barrett Browning had nothing on me. Sam, I didn't think that the poem was all that good either and I was slightly disappointed in the standards of the school district. Dad said that I should have tried a lot harder, since I only got a blue ribbon for coming in second. Emma did the whole flower collection for Pam and she never let me live down the fact that her grade was higher than mine.

Yes, the visit with Hank was just great, but we were all Mona'd out after a few hours, especially Dad. Hank is just the best and I wish we'd get to see him more than just every four years or so. Mona is nothing but a spoiled child, but Hank adores her and waits on her hand and foot. Sam, I agree with you. I didn't think that Mona treated her daughters very nicely either. It's not that she was over-protective, which she was to a fault, but it seemed to me that in spite of all the attention she paid to the girls, she was, deep down, a little indifferent. After Grace graduated from high school, she went to secretarial school and started working for a law firm. After doing that for a few months, she suddenly announced to Hank and Mona that she was getting married, which came as a great surprise to them, since they weren't even aware of the fact that she was dating. Six months after the wedding, Grace gave birth to a little girl. Mona told us and, I am sure everyone else, that it was a very premature birth. Sam, give me a break. The baby weighed nine pounds. Hank did not care at all that Grace had to get married and he was overjoyed with his granddaughter and ecstatic about Grace finally being happy. He sent us quite a few pictures of himself, proudly holding that little bundle. I looked at all the pictures and noticed every detail and I have to agree with you, Sam. He and I look very much alike, but what exactly did you mean when you said that we resembled each other very much, except that he was a lot better looking? In what way? And how could he be better looking when you had just said that we looked so much alike? As you can see, Honey, I am perfectly capable of ignoring your remark about my looks. I think that Monica is about ready to graduate from high school. Don't know what her plans for the future are, but she might very well follow in her sister's footsteps.

Sam, I asked Dad a little while ago about "it" and "twice". He was very baf-fled (his word, Sam, not mine) that I did not remember "Thrice" in one night. Brian, Sweetheart, I love you, but you're full of it.

CHAPTER 26

❀

(May)

It's about two o'clock in the morning. Got home about an hour ago, talked to Mom and Dad for a few minutes, took a bath and went to bed. Once I was I bed I didn't know what I was doing there, since I was not in the least sleepy, so I got up, turned on the stereo, and got my diary out and am I the mood to write about tonight, the big junior-senior prom. Think I am on my fourth diary now. Mom happily buys them for me.

Dean picked up Pam at six and they came back to the house and let Dad take some pictures of them, the three of us and then just me and Dean. Pam looked absolutely gorgeous and Dean was no slouch either in a black tux. He had rented some black patent leather shoes to go with the tux, but at the last minute he decided that he wasn't going to wear those sissy tap dance shoes and he wore his boots.

Alan was picking me up at seven. He and I had to go through the whole picture taking rigmarole. Alan looked real nice in his tux and he gave me a pretty wrist corsage and I was thinking why I could not feel a little more excited about it all. He took me to a restaurant where we had dinner with two other couples from school. The prom started at eight, but we didn't get there till much later. There was a live band and they were good and they played a lot of different music. Guess they wanted to please everyone. The first couple on the dance floor was none other than Dean and Pam. She was twirling Dean around like there was no tomorrow and he was laughing and he looked so happy and he never took his eyes off Pam.

I danced a lot with Alan, who is pretty good and so much better than I am. I am just not a Jennifer Grey, although I come close to dancing like her when I am alone in my room. I also danced with some other guys and then Dean asked me and he was so sweet. Come to think of it, he has been pretty nice to me ever since he started dating Pam. A bunch of girls who did not have a date showed up together and I thought that was pretty neat. They seemed to be having a good time, probably a better time than some of the people out there tonight. Not having a date to the prom is one thing, but at least they didn't sit at home moping about it. I don't think I'd have the guts to do that. Think I would just stay home and feel sorry for myself.

The prom was over at midnight and then about eight of us decided to go to an all-night restaurant for breakfast, which sounded like fun. Dean saw us leave and he pulled me aside and told me to remember what Mom and Dad had talked to me about. What is he, my father? Alan was driving and we gave another couple, Gary and Stephanie, a ride. As soon as we got in the car, Gary, a senior and a real geek, asked Alan where the booze was and Alan told him it was under the seat. It wasn't just a flask, it was a huge bottle. He took a swallow and passed it to Stephanie. She's in one of my classes and she's a royal pain in the ass. She took the bottle of stinky smelling crap from Gary, drank some and said, "Oh. That's so good. I've been waiting for this all evening," in what she probably thought was a real sexy voice, but she sounded just plain stupid. Then she passed the bottle to Alan and I was waiting for him to say that he didn't want any, but he took a long drink and said, "Good brand, Gary" as if he was an expert on the subject of hard liquor, and, he too, sounded plain stupid. All I wanted to tell Alan was, "I have known you for years and I've always liked you as a friend. I am so pissed at myself for being such a poor judge of character, because I just realize that I've been running around with nothing but an easily-influenced piece of shit." Then Alan passed the bottle to me and all I could think of was Mom and Dad and what they told me before Alan picked me up. Dad gave me a hug, hoped that I would have a wonderful time and gave me a 2:00 AM curfew, which was later than I had hoped for. Mom put in her two cents worth and said that she trusted me implicitly, and that if I didn't know right from wrong by now, I was never going to get the concept. She also said that she knew I didn't drink, except an occasional sip of beer at home and, of course, the Kahlua, but that she would absolutely not condone me touching any liquor tonight and nor was I to ride in a vehicle with anybody who had recently had a drink. Recently meaning within the past five days. I told Mom to stop worrying and that I had no desire to drink and, as far as I knew, Alan didn't drink either. All these thoughts went through my head when Alan passed me the bottle and I hated him for putting me in that position, but I told him that I was not interested. We had a quick breakfast, not quick enough for me, and then Alan and Gary wanted to hang around a supermarket and wait for someone they knew and who was old enough to buy them a bottle of wine and I had it. Asked Alan to take me home and that stupid twit, Stephanie, said she could not believe that anyone our age had to have a curfew. I hope they found someone to buy them a bottle and I hope they drank it all and I hope that they all puked their brains out. Anyway, Alan drove me home and Gary and the girl with the I.Q. of a crouton waited at the restaurant for him to get back. Think that Alan was in a big hurry to get back, because he drove way too fast. He was so rude and didn't even wait for me to get inside. Alan, I did not do you any justice. You are not a piece of shit. You are the embodiment of a perfect asshole.

Dean was already in bed when I got home. Too bad, because I wanted to ask him how he had liked the prom. I thought it was great, but I could well have done without all the crap afterwards. Don't think that Alan will call me any time soon. Hope not. I also want to ask Dean if he knows Gary and if he hates him as much as I do, which is a considerable amount.

It sure is nice to be home. Am so glad that we didn't get stopped by the police and sorry that I didn't tell Stephanie to "go fuck herself." Hope she'll give me another chance to do that. I am sure that Mom will have a million questions tomorrow. She was too sleepy when I got home and only asked if I had a good time.

(Later)

It's Monday evening and I don't have time to write very long, because I have a lot of studying to do. Just want to write one thing down.

In the lunch room in school today, Pam told me that Dean is suspended from school for two days. He evidently had a fight with Gary in the hall and he broke his tooth. Since Dean started it, he had to go to the principal. Webster told him that he might not suspend him if Dean gave him the whole story, but Dean had no intention. I never had a chance to ask Dean yesterday what he thought of Gary, but I guess I don't have to anymore. When I got home from school today, Mom had just had a phone call from Webster, informing her that her son was not welcome in school until Thursday. She wasn't upset at all. Mom tried to talk to him when he got home, but he wasn't very informative. He said "yes" when she asked him if he felt that he had an excellent and justifiable reason for starting a fight and "no" when she asked him if he thought she was unreasonable in suggesting that he pay for half of Gary's dental bill when he had his tooth bonded and she and Dad would pay the rest. Mom did not want me to pester Dean with an abundance of questions, but I figured that "abundance" did not mean that I could not ask him one, eency-weency question and I did, but Dean said that, of course, him hitting the crap out of Gary had nothing to do with me. I gave him a hug, just in case he was not telling me the truth. He's so lucky. He called the ranch and he's going to get a lot of hours in the next two days. Mom told him that, if he wanted to, she'd take him to his favorite barbeque place for lunch and Dean said they had a deal. Honestly, please give me a break. Here he gets suspended from school for two days and she's taking him out for lunch? Is that punishment or what.

❀   ❀   ❀

Sam, Sweetheart, I know how annoyed and unpleasantly surprised you and Dean sometimes were when I found out things that you had done or said, matters that you didn't want anyone to know, especially not your mother. What happened to me after the prom? Was I losing this ability, this gift? Must have, because I never had an inkling about all the goings-on after the prom. Sam, I am proud of you for not giving in to peer pressure and yes, thank God that you were not stopped by the police. However, I am a tad disappointed in you for not speaking your mind and telling Stephanie what she could do to herself.

Sam, Dean was pretty passive and no more interested in fighting than a missionary and I deducted that he, who had never caused any problems in school, must have had a good reason for starting a fight. I had never given Dean's suspension much thought until I read about the prom night, and now I am curious. I just asked Dad and he knew all about it, but he just never bothered to divulge any information to me until now. You should be proud of Dean. Gary evidently made a derogatory remark about you and your unwillingness to drink and have a good time and Dean took up for you and, as you would say, beat the crap out of him. Oh, Sam, I hope you already knew all that and it bothers me that I'll never know for sure. Not only did I take Dean out for lunch that day, I also bought him two pair of jeans. Do you think that was ample punishment? Had I known then what I know now, I would have thrown in some shirts. Before I go to bed tonight, I am going to write Dean a check for fifty dollars, which was his contribution for having that ass's tooth repaired.

CHAPTER 27

❀

(June)

I am home by myself and I feel like writing. Yeah!!! Summer has started and no school for almost two months. I am going to work in the "Three in One" again, but am not starting until Monday, so I have four whole days to myself. Am looking forward to working and I hope I like it as much as last year. The place still has the same manager and she and I get along great.

Let's see what happened. Dean graduated a week ago. They had the ceremony on the football field and it was beautiful. When I saw Dean in his cap and gown I was thinking about graduating myself, which is just one year away. Dean was in the top five of his class and that's really something. Mom tries not to brag about him too much, but she cannot help herself.

Grandma and Grandpa flew over for the occasion. I went to the airport to pick them up and Grandma told me that I was driving too fast, even though everybody was passing us. Grandpa thought that I was driving too slowly, since every car on the road was passing me, and said that it wouldn't hurt to speed it up a little. He's so sweet.

Mom and Dad wanted to give Dean a big party, but he was dead set against it, so she fixed a nice buffet dinner for everybody. Pam's mother was sick and couldn't make it. Pam came, of course, and so did her sisters, some people that Mom and Dad knew and a lot of Dean's friends. And, guess who also showed up? None other than John Griffin, the love of my life. Too bad he doesn't know that. He didn't stay very long, but we did talk and I hope I didn't sound like a moron. I hope he's in one of my classes again in the fall. I forgot to mention, and what an oversight that was, that John was at the prom, but he didn't stay long. I didn't know the girl he was with. Don't think she goes to our school. Maybe, just maybe, it was his sister.

After Dean left to get ready for graduation, I asked Mom if she didn't think that John was awfully good looking. She thought he was. Also said that if I had been willing to give up part of some Saturdays and go to track meets, I could have seen him in action. Then to really rub it in, she added that he has nice legs and an even cuter butt.

Like I said. The ceremony was on the football field. Grandma wasn't too happy about having to sit on the bleachers and she complained to Mom about the sun being in her eyes. Mom told her that she felt personally responsible for a lot of things in life, but that she was not to blame for the sun setting in the west. Grandma gave her a dirty look, which she completely ignored. Good for you, Mom. The valedictorian's speech was not all that great, at least I didn't think so. I sure hope that Pam is going to be valedictorian at our graduation. The ceremony was nice and I felt pretty proud when they called out Dean's name and I think that Mom was sniffling. Dean got home shortly after we did, just to change his clothes and then he and Pam were going to some place close to the lake, where they had an all-night sponsored party for all the graduates and their dates.

He said he'd be home around eight the next morning, but he walked in around one o'clock. Dad and Grandpa had already gone to bed, Mom and I were cleaning up the kitchen and Grandma was reading. I asked Mom why Grandma stayed up so friggin' late and Mom said that Grandma was afraid she might miss something if she retired early. Anyway, when Mom heard Dean pull up in the driveway, she said, "Oh holy shit, I hope nothing has happened." Grandma asked Mom if she couldn't think of a better way to express her concerns. Mom told me that she could think of a better way, but it involved the "F" word and she didn't think that Grandma was ready for that. Dean said that Pam was not feeling well at all and they decided to go home. Mom said that she might be getting the same thing as Emma, but Dean said that it was not a bad summer cold, just a case of "Francine's syndrome." Mom and I started laughing and I asked Dean if he knew what it was. Since he didn't say "yes" or "no" we decided that it was high time to educate him. We had a girl, Francine, in our sophomore class. Whenever she had not done her homework or was unprepared for a test, which was quite often, she would blame it on her period. It was getting to the point where we all thought she had a period just about every ten days or so and we started referring to it as "Francine's syndrome" and we still call it that. Dean said that he figured that, but Mom and I weren't so sure. Mom put her arms around Dean and told Dean that even his girlfriend on the pedestal suffered from mundane things, such as a period. For some reason, Grandma did not know what we were talking about and she wanted to know what was wrong with that "charming young lady". Mom said that she just had her period. Grandma told Mom that she could not believe that we discussed menstruation in front of Dean. Mom rolled her eyes and Grandma noticed it. Mom quickly rubbed her eyes and said that the pollen in the air was just killing her. Then Dean told Grandma that we discuss a lot of topics in this family, such as abortion, AIDS and birth control and he asked me and Mom if he had forgotten anything. I added pre-marital sex and pedophilia and Mom came up with communicable diseases, necrophilia, and emotional abuse. I think she threw that last one in just for Grandma, who treats Mom like shit.

Dean got a four-year scholarship to Baylor in Waco. He wants to be an electrical engineer. He wants to go to summer school every year and graduate in three years. More power to him. I know he'll do it. He is going to share a very small, two-bedroom apartment. It's going to be so strange without him. I never thought I would miss him, but I am going to very much. Hope he thinks about me a little from time to time. Pam said that she is going to miss him so badly.

Pam has decided that she wants to major in sociology when she goes to college. In many ways, she's so very much like Dean. They both know exactly what they want to do with their life. Pam's lowest grade last year was 101 and she's either first or second in class ranking. She's so modest and never talks about it. She wants to go to Baylor to be with Dean. Think I mentioned earlier that I have no clue about what I want to major in. My grades are good, all A's and an occasional B, but I don't know what I am really good in. Mom told me that it is hard to decide what you want to do when you're so good in many fields and that's why I cannot make up my mind. As much as I like English, I don't think that I want to study it for four years. I like writing, but I don't want to be a writer and for that, I'd probably have to major in English and I already said that I don't want to do that. Whatever, I have another year of high school and maybe during that year I'll get a better idea.

Let me see. What else has happened. Dean has his own car now, a pickup and he spends a lot of time in and on it. It's a year old and it was a graduation present from Mom and Dad. I've never seen Dean so excited as he was on the day that he and Dad drove it home, about a month before graduation. As soon as he dropped Dad off, he went to Pam's to show her his prize possession and said that he was now able to take her out in style. Pam told him that the truck was nice-looking, but that she really didn't care what he drove. As far as she was concerned, he could pick her up on a bicycle, just as long as he showed up. The car that Dean and I shared fell apart and Dad said that it was not worth getting it fixed up. Last month I drove Mom's car a lot, but that didn't work out very well. I asked Mom why she was so reluctant about me driving her car and she said that it had something to do with empty soda cans, gum wrappers, McDonald's bags, sitting on a French fry, a dirty hairbrush and an empty tank. Well, yes, I can see her point. Think that Mom complained to Dad, because one day he came home with a four-door Chevrolet with 88,000 miles on it. It may not be the best-looking car, but it is all mine and I couldn't be happier with it. I'll get a different vehicle next spring, assuming I can come up with the amount of money I am supposed to come up with. I had better check my savings book to see how much I saved last summer. I would dearly love to check my savings book, but I have no idea where it is. Maybe I should call the bank. I just did and my balance is not exactly what I was hoping it was. I told the person who answered the phone that I was very disappointed in the amount and she said that she hears that a lot. I am not too worried about it. Will make and save a lot this summer. Pam is going to work in the same restaurant as last year. Last summer she swore that she was never going to be a waitress again, but she changed her mind because the tips were so good. She also starts on Monday. She has irregular hours and is afraid that she's not going to see much of Dean, because he's going to take nine hours this summer and also work at the ranch. I told Pam that she had nothing to worry about and that she'll probably see him more this summer than when he was still in high school.

Grandma and Grandpa flew back to Seattle the Monday after graduation. Dean was working, Dad had to go to the office early, so that left Mom to drive them to the airport. Mom asked me if I would please, please, pretty please, go with her and I went. We dropped them off at departures. Grandpa was sweet to Mom. Gave her a big kiss and thanked her for everything. Grandma just said, "Well, goodbye, Helen," and didn't hug Mom. Mom was pretty big and I was proud of her. She gave Grandma a very quick hug, said it had been good to see her and thanked her for her generosity. I missed first period and part of second, but that didn't matter. It's the end of school and there's not much going on. Mom dropped me off at school and when she drove off I yelled at her that I didn't have an absence note. She rolled down the window and yelled at me to go for it, since I copy her handwriting so well.

I forgot to mention something. Grandma and Grandpa gave Dean a big check to "further his education", as Grandma called it. The day after they left,

Dean asked Mom if she thought that a stereo for his pickup came under furthering his education. Mom said, "absolutely"and so did a crow bar (she meant roll bar), an amplifier and whatever else he wanted for the truck. Dean bought everything the next day and in the evening, he and Dad installed it all.

Pam called a few minutes ago. She's coming to pick me up and we're going to get a pizza.

      ❧   ❧   ❧

Dad and I were so proud of Dean. When he walked on the stage to receive his diploma, he looked so self-assured and confident. He also looked so very handsome and he was beginning to look more and more like Dad. There was no doubt in my or Dad's mind that he wouldn't reach all the goals he had set for himself. Throughout the ceremony I was thinking about how much I loved Dean, about how much I would miss him when he went off to college and about how I was ever going to stop those tears from running down my cheeks. Sam, I was not sniffling. I was crying. There's a distinct difference.

A couple of months ago, we had one of Dad's associates and his wife, Mary, over for dinner. Their daughter was then a freshman in college and Mary said that it was a very traumatic experience and that this trauma included feelings of loneliness and abandonment, the fear of being unable to cope successfully with new developments and situations, a certain amount of insecurity and the realization that you are not quite as prepared as you had thought you were. Mary, who was a little full of herself, sounded like she was reading from the "Ladies' Home Journal" and I didn't pay as much attention to her words as I probably should have. I didn't know if she was talking about her own feelings or about her daughter's, but I felt a little of all the above after Dean left. The day Dean left for summer school, I could not stop hugging and holding him. He got impatient and said, "Stop it, Mom. It's no big deal. I'll see you next week-end." and he hardly ever missed a week. I realize that if it had not been for Pam, he might have found a job in Waco and we'd hardly ever see him. Just one more reason for me and Dad to like and love Pam.

Sam, you're right. Grandma didn't treat me nicely at all. When she was not ignoring me, she would make derogatory remarks either to my face or behind my back, but only when Dad was not around and that's why I asked him one time not to leave my side too often and he didn't. Dad hardly ever mentions her and I don't think that he's very fond of her. He always took up for me when she slipped and said something negative about me in front of him and so did

Grandpa. Grandpa even told her to "lay off" one time when she went too far. I always called Grandpa by his first name, "Harold," and I felt comfortable doing so. Grandma never told me how I should or could address her, so I called her "Hi, how are you" when she arrived and during her visit I managed not to call her anything. The Sunday after graduation, Emma, who was feeling better, came over for a few minutes. She had talked to Grandma over the phone a few times, but had never met her in person. Emma waltzed through the door, shook Grandma's hand and asked Grandma what she wanted to be called. Grandma said, "Emma, you could honor me by calling me "Loretta." If I had asked Grandma that question, she would more than likely have said, "Helen, you could honor me by calling me "Mrs. Evers." so I am glad I never asked her. Of course, after Emma left, I had to listen to Grandma going on and on about what a charming, beautiful and delightful lady Emma was. I told Emma about that the next day and she laughed and said, "Well, fuck me. Didn't know your mother-in-law was so observant." Enough about Grandma. If I dwell on her peculiarities and meanness any longer I am going to get angry and she's not worth it.

CHAPTER 28

❀

(July)

This summer is going by too fast and I cannot believe that school will start again in just a few weeks. I am ready for my senior year and looking forward to graduating and going to college. Have given a lot of thought to majoring in English and it's beginning to appeal to me. Wouldn't mind teaching at a high school and make it as interesting as Mrs. Sellers. I discussed it with Mom and Dad. They said that it didn't matter all that much to them what I was going to major in, just as long as it made me happy. Anyway, I am glad that I am fairly positive about what I want to do, but I am not ruling out changing my mind sometime this coming year.

Have all my clothes ready for school. I used my discount at the "Three in One" and bought a lot of outfits and Mom reimbursed me for most of them. All that's left is shopping for shoes and I hate to even think about it. I may just buy a couple of pairs of comfortable sneakers and say to hell with the other kinds. Oh shit, I just started my period. Just checked my bathroom and Mom's and we're pretty low on Tampax, so I'd best run over to the supermarket and get some. I hate to buy them. Every time I get ready to check out an economy size box, the regular checker goes on a break, and the new checker is a guy I know from school and I never find it necessary for him to know that I have "Francine's syndrome". Heard that Francine is not coming back this year. Some kids say that she was pregnant, but that was just gossip. Well, if she is pregnant, at least she doesn't have to worry about having a period every ten days.

(Later)

Just got back from the supermarket and yes, I feel much better now, thank you very much. Pam and I drove to Waco a few weeks ago. Dean's apartment is tiny, but he's got it all organized and he's pretty proud of it. Pam had seen it at the beginning of summer and thought it looked drab. She took the sizes of the windows, went to Walmart where she bought some cheap, but cheerful-looking material and gave it to me. She thought that since I had taken a semester of home economics, I should be able to make some curtains. I told her that I wasn't about to, but that I knew just the woman to take on this task, my mother. Mom made us cut the material and pin the seams and hems and then she sewed them and then Pam ironed them, because they were a mess. Mom asked Pam to tell Dean not ever to wash them, because since she had not basted them, they might ravel. Pam told Mom that she didn't have to worry about that. Anyway, they looked pretty nice. Dean finished summer school and made two A's and a B. Pretty damned good, considering he also worked a lot of hours at the ranch.

Alan and I have been dating a little this summer, but nothing serious. We're just friends and we'll never be more than that. After the prom, I swore that I would never talk to him again. It took him about two months to apologize for being such a creep and, by that time, I was a little over my disgust. I told him that if he ever drank in front of me again or if he made me run around with others who were drinking, I'd kill him. When he said that he knew he'd made a fool of himself, I rolled my eyes. I caught myself doing it and I thought, "Oh God, I am so much like my mother." Alan must have noticed the rolling of the eyes, because he quickly changed the "fool" to "insensitive asshole." After he said that he had really missed our friendship, which he had taken for granted, I sorta mellowed and we started going out again. Like Mom often says, "There's a sucker born every minute." I know he likes me, but I am not stupid and I know that he'd drop me in a second if he fell in love, but then I would do the same. Still, I think that even if that happened, we'd still be friends. I would like nothing better than finding someone who looks at me the way Dad looks at Mom and Dean at Pam.

Mom and I were talking about dating not too long ago and she told me not to worry too much about not having a steady boyfriend. She said that she could count the dates she had all through high school on the fingers of one hand. Finally, in her senior year she met someone and fell madly in love with him. I asked her how long they dated and she said that, since it all happened so long ago, she could not quite remember, but she thought it might have been as long as a month. She dated him for four weeks and that is what she considered the love of her life? Talking about dating. Mom asked me the other day if I had any idea how involved Dean and Pam were with each other. I told her that they were pretty serious about each other, and I wanted to leave it at that, but that didn't satisfy her. Mom thinks the world of Pam and she said that she could not think of a better, nicer and sweeter girl for Dean, but she also wished that they would start seeing other people. Then she had the absolute nerve to ask me if I knew if they had been sleeping together. I am pretty sure they have, but Pam has never mentioned it and I am not about to ask her. I told Mom that I had no idea if they've done it once or twice. She put her head down on the table and whispered, "You mean to tell me that they may have done it more than once?" She is afraid that they might be getting entirely too serious and thinks that they're both too young to get all involved and wish they would wait until after they both graduate from college. I told Mom that she was pretty old farty and old fashioned and she didn't like that one bit. I told her that times have changed since she was a teenager and she didn't quite agree with that state-ment. She thinks that my generation is conning hers into accepting new ideas and beliefs, which are sometimes far from desirable, but they are reluctantly accepted out for fear of being called old-fashioned. She thinks that we, kids my age, as a result of the doubtful benefit of modern technology, such as stereos, VCR's, DVD's and the like, have become lazy and taciturn and have lost the ability or inclination to communicate openly. Also, according to her, most teenagers have a ready supply of available cash, handed to them by their par-ents, and giving them a sense of false financial security. I don't know if I wrote down everything correctly, but that was the gist of it. All of this made me think a little and I told Mom that I kinda understood what she was saying, but that I didn't agree with everything she had said. She said that I had a right to my own opinion, and then she suggested that we go out and get some ice cream. I was all for it, because for a moment I didn't think that she was ever going to shut up on the subject of the generation gap. I suggested that we might want to go out for yogurt instead of ice cream, because ice cream makes her whine. Mom said that I was right. Whenever she eats ice cream I have to listen to what it might do to her butt and how mad she is at herself for not exercising any self-control and ordering three scoops instead of one. Then, when we get home, she puts on her jogging clothes and runs for half an hour, trying to work off the calories. If it happens to be dark, she wants me or Dean to go with her. I hate jogging. It's a stupid thing to do. Dean loves it, but he doesn't like to go with her. He did it one time and that was enough for him. Mom tried to talk and run at the same time, but she got out of breath and told Dean, "To hell with running. Let's just talk." Dean did not think that talking gave him any exercise, but Mom told him that his vocal cords were more in need of exercising than his legs were.

Pam's sister turned sixteen earlier this summer and her dad bought her and her sister a car, as promised. He took Kim and Joyce away for a few days and when they got back, he and Pam bought a car, which is worse-looking than mine. Pam said that he only paid nine hundred dollars for it and that she wanted to throw up when he pulled out this wad of money and peeled off nine one hundred dollar bills. She doesn't like her dad. When Pam showed me the car, she said that she was not in the best of moods and that she felt depressed. I thought that she was upset with that piece of crap of a car, but she said that didn't matter all that much and that she was happy with it as long as it got her from one place to another and we both thought that wouldn't be for very long. She was pissed at her dad. He has a new girlfriend and she came with him on this short trip. She is about twenty-two and kinda pretty in a stupid way and she was trying very hard to make herself popular with Pam and her sisters and Pam hated her the moment she set eyes on her. Her dad is forty-four and Pam said that he's trying to act much younger and that he dresses like a nerd, has his shirt half-open, gold chains dangling everywhere and long hair. Pam said that her mother was furious when she drove home in that shitty-looking car, because she knew that he drives a Jaguar and that he always bought his bimbos something foreign and expensive and she thought that he could have done better for his daughters. When Pam's dad gave her a goodbye kiss, he quickly told her to tell their mother that he was getting married and Pam got mad at him and told him that he should be the one to tell her, but he wasn't going to. Pam postponed it as long as she could and waited for a good time to tell her, but, of course, there was no good time. When Pam finally told her, her mother calmly told her that she was not too surprised. She asked Pam if she seemed nice and Pam told her that she sucked majorly and Emma said that was exactly what she wanted to hear. And then she asked Pam how old his latest flame was and that was the question Pam didn't want to answer, so she just said, "Just a little younger than he is, Mom." Emma didn't buy it and wanted to know exactly how much younger and Pam said, "Maybe she's just a little more than just a little younger than he is, Mom", which was a badly-constructed sentence coming from the smartest person I know. When Pam's mother told her, "Out with it,

Pam", and Pam said, "about twenty years", her mother got so mad she almost started hyperventilating and it scared Pam to death.

Pam's and Joyce's car started falling apart after about two weeks. Dad and Dean worked on it. They changed the oil, put new fan belts in and some other things and it drove all right for a while. Then one day, when Pam was on her way to work, it stopped in the middle of the highway and she called me to pick her up. Someone helped us push it over to the side of the road and that's where we left it. Pam's mother refused to call a wrecker, because she was afraid that he would charge more than the car was worth. Later that day, Dad towed it to a garage. They called Pam's mother and told her how much it was going to cost to get it all fixed and Pam's mother called him a "fucking cheater". Then she felt ashamed of herself, called the guy back and apologized. Think she told the guy that her outburst was due to an extreme case of frustration, brought on by this assholic ex-husband, who was the dick of all dicks. Then she asked Pam if she should call him back again and tell him she was sorry about using words like "assholic" and "dick" and Pam told her to forget it, because she might end up having to call him several more times. Pam told me this whole story and we couldn't stop laughing.

Not much else going on. I have not saved as much this summer as I should have, but I still think that I am going to have enough for a down payment on a decent, used car next year. I want a two-door, preferably a convertible and bright red. I asked Mom what she thought of that and she said that the only thing she liked were the two doors. Dad has been very busy. He used to get home around five or so, but lately it has been much later. They started construction on a medical building that Dad's company designed and that's keeping them busy.

Best close for now. Pam is coming over pretty soon. Dean should be here any minute. I am going to ask Mom if she wants me to pick up some hamburgers. She doesn't like cooking and she'll probably give me a hug and say, "Thank you, Honey. Thought you'd never offer." I was right, but she didn't have any money, so I'll have to pay for it.

❦   ❦   ❦

Sam, that was the best summer. Everybody was content and busy. You were working at the "Three in One", Dean was doing very well in summer school, working and seeing Pam, Dad was having some difficulties with the medical building, but, since he thrived on solving problems, he was happy and I had a great time painting the interior of our house.

Sam, you were right. I was getting more than just a little concerned about Dean and Pam, and so was Emma. Dean had three years of college ahead of him and Pam still had one year of high school. Pam had the brains to be accepted in any university and Emma was afraid that she might lose her desire to go and marry Dean after her senior year, not that marriage had ever been mentioned. Emma and Pam had a very good daughter-mother relationship and they had no trouble discussing any subject, with the exception of dating. Whenever Emma brought up Dean's name, Pam thought that she might be in for a long tirade and she would cut Emma short by saying, "Jeez, mother, we are only dating", something Emma was fully aware of. Dean wasn't anymore informative when I approached the subject and he asked to be left alone. Dad took Emma and me out for dinner one evening and Emma talked Dad into ordering some wine. Needless to say, we discussed Pam and Dean. Dad said that he didn't understand our concern. He thought that Dean might meet some nice girls in college and Pam might find someone in her senior year. Emma and I looked at him for a long time and then Emma said, "Brian, I've known you for many years and I think the world of you. However, I don't know if it was you or that one puny glass of wine talking. Whatever it was, it was a real dumb-ass remark." Until she uttered that sentence, Dad had participated very nicely in the conversation, but after that he became more of a very patient listener.

Whenever I bugged Dean with questions about Pam, I felt truly ashamed of myself, but not ashamed enough to stop pestering him altogether. I would look up at this handsome, intelligent and wonderful young man, who had never given us anything but happiness since the day he was born and I thought that I, even though I was his mother, had no right to meddle in his affairs, but sometimes I just could not help myself. Dean, Honey, I don't know if you're ever going to read this, but if you do, please forgive me for having irritated you occasionally from time to time. There was no excuse for that, except that I am your mother and maybe I was going through the change of life. Truthfully, I had not approached that stage in life yet, but two excuses were better than none. Dean reminded me so much of Dad and I thought that if Dean was going to be half the husband and father that Dad was, his wife and children were truly blessed.

That summer was not one of Emma's happiest. She was upset with her ex-husband. They had been divorced for almost ten years, but still, she deeply resented the fact that he was taking more than a casual interest in someone twenty years his junior and when she found out that they had gotten married, she almost fell to pieces. Emma did not have a high opinion of her ex, but she didn't want him to get re-married before she did. I think that Emma, deep down, very, very, deep down never stopped caring about the S.O.B. Also, Emma was getting tired of having the sole responsibility of raising three teenage daughters and I didn't blame her. She was anxious to find someone with whom to share her menopause years, but there was one obstacle in her way and that was the availability of eligible men between the age of forty and fifty. Emma finally met someone, Ken, at a party that summer and she thought that he had distinct possibilities. She had that thought before she even had a cocktail and she found that a good omen for a long-lasting relationship. He called her a few days after the party and invited her out for dinner. Emma was dying to go, but she declined, because her youngest daughter had a stomach virus and Emma didn't want to leave her, so she asked Ken over and fixed him dinner. She said that he was a real gentleman and her two youngest really liked him. They went out several more times and then he treated her for dinner at a very exclusive restaurant and Emma liked his extravagance. They had a wonderful evening until the waiter walked up and asked them if they were ready to order dessert. Ken leered at Emma, pinched her thigh under the table, which pissed Emma off big time, as you would have said, Sam, and told the waiter that they were going to have dessert at his place and Emma knew that he was not talking about a slice of cheesecake. Emma felt furious and humiliated and excused herself and called home. Joyce answered the phone and she was pretty disappointed that her mother had not gotten engaged that evening. Pam was not at home. Emma called our house and asked me to pick her up a block away from the restaurant and I did. I felt so sorry for Emma. She is such a good person and such a great friend and I just wanted her to be happy.

Yes, that first car that Emma's ex bought for his two daughters left much to be desired. Emma called him. She never told anyone what she told him over the phone, but it must have been very effective, because within a week, she received a note and a substantial check. She cashed the check, withheld a little for herself, just a token payment for all the "bastard" had put her through and told Pam and Joyce to go out and buy a good used car. Dad and Dean went with them and they bought something Japanese and Pam and her sister were thrilled with it.

CHAPTER 29

❀

(September)

God, I am so glad that this week is over. It's almost the end of the first six weeks. My classes are really tough this year and I am having a little trouble with analytic geometry. Had a test in it today and could have used Dad's help, but he was out of town. Mom offered her help. She looked at the book and handed it back. She said that since she did not understand the chapter headings, she would be of little help to me. Called some kids in my class, but they were also lost. Called Dean and he helped me over the phone and then I called some people in my class back and explained it to them. By the time I had done that five times, I understood it. Think that I did pretty well on the test after all. Pam and I have Spanish II together and it's a breeze and my easiest class this semester.

Dean started college the week before we did. He is taking eighteen hours and still finds time to run in the evening. Beats the hell out of me why he likes running so much. Pam asked me to go to Waco with her one day and I met Dean's roommate. His name is Sidney. He's from New Jersey and he's funny and nice as anything and Dean really likes him which is saying quite a lot. Dean stays in Waco Friday night and studies, drives home early on Saturday, works at the ranch, and takes Pam out in the evening. Drives back on Sunday, just as soon as all his laundry is clean, folded and ironed. I do most of that and I don't mind. He had an awful lot of laundry last week-end and when I said something, Dean said that some of it might be Sidney's, which had accidentally gotten mixed up with his. Mom thought that was a very likely story and she bought a big laundry bag and told Dean it was a present for Sidney and that we

(We? Where did she get that "We?") would be happy to do his laundry too and that he was welcome here anytime.

I am still playing basketball and I still love it as much as the day I started. We have a pretty good team this year. We added a new girl. She just moved here from Houston and she is the best player on our team. Hope we win the state championship this year. We came very close last year, but then we screwed up in the end.

Mom is on her way to the airport to get Dad. Pam is coming over later. Think we're either going to hang out here or at her house. I may as well keep writing until she gets here. I have been waking up with a headache every morning for about a week now and I am getting sick of it. Taking aspirin seems to help most of the time. Mom thinks I am studying too hard (me?) and am too busy with school and basketball and that I am not getting enough rest. She wants me to get my eyes checked in a week or so if I am still complaining. She said that I ve been squinting a lot lately when I am reading. She is pretty sure that I need glasses and that the headaches will disappear.

❀   ❀   ❀

Yes, Sam, you were near-sighted and needed glasses, but I was so wrong about the headaches going away.

CHAPTER 30

❀

(September again)

There's a lot to write about. I got my glasses and they look pretty good. I got several pairs, since I am afraid I might lose one. I don't mind wearing them at all. My headaches went away for a couple of days. Dad said that I can order contact lenses, if I want to, but I really don't care.

I am going to have dinner at Pam's Friday evening and then we're going to a *Linkin Park* concert in San Antonio. This guy in our Spanish class had some extra tickets and sold them to us real cheap. Pam and I never liked him all that much, but after he sold, practically gave, us the tickets, we like him a lot better.

(Later)

I had a terrible headache in school this morning and I even went to the nurse's office to lie down. The nurse asked me all sorts of questions about my period. She asks all the girls about their period, no matter what they are complaining about, and she takes everybody's temperature. I don't think she's all that good, but she is sweet to all the kids and she listens to people's problems. Anyway, after a while, my headache went away and I went back to class.

Towards the end of fourth period, they announced over the intercom that I had to go to the office. Mom was there and she had already signed me out. Obviously, the nurse was concerned and she called home and Mom probably became agitated and panicky, like she does so well, and she made an appointment with the doctor. I got a little p.o.'d at her in the car and told her that I was old enough to go to the doctor by myself, but she only said, "Be that as it may." That did not make much sense to me, but I was not about to ask her, because her explanation might be just as incoherent as her statement and she would still go to the doctor with me anyway, so I didn't waste my breath.

The doctor gave me a physical and could not find anything wrong with me. That did not surprise me at all. I've never been sick a day in my life, except for the annual cold, measles and other childhood diseases. Then he asked Mom to come to his office and he recommended that I have some tests taken at the hospital and see a neurologist and he set it all up for tomorrow. I whispered to Mom that I had two tests tomorrow and that I could not miss school, and she didn't even bother to whisper, but said out loud, "I don't give a continental fart about your tests." I told her later that she sounded just like Pam's mother and she laughed and said that Emma was definitely a very good mentor.

When we got home, Mom called Dad and told him about the upcoming tests. She hardly ever calls him at the office, so I guess she was a little worried. I am not at all. All the test results will be negative and it is just going to be a big waste of money. Meanwhile, I don't know how long it's going to take tomorrow and what time we'll get back, so maybe I should stop writing and start studying for the two tests. I hate make-up tests. They always seem harder and that's not right, especially if you have a good excuse for not taking them the first time.

(Later)

Well, I had a CAT scan, skull X-rays, an MRI and other tests today and that just about took most of the day. Since school was already out, Mom took me out for an early dinner and I sucked her into buying me a pair of jeans. We'll get all the results of the tests on Monday.

❧   ❧   ❧

Sam, when we left the doctor's office that day, my hart was palpitating more than it should and I had a terrible premonition that something might be seriously wrong with you. I tried to put on a good show reassuring you that these tests were just routine, but it didn't ease my mind. You didn't seem overly concerned, to say the least, only upset that you had missed school and had to take the tests the following day. I believe that I only talked to hear my own voice and I was trying so hard to convince myself that you were as healthy as always, but I must not have done a good job, because I continued to have this gnawing and uneasy feeling in the pit of my stomach.

That night, after you went to bed, I fixed a big pot of coffee and Dad and I talked for hours. He told me that I had always had a tendency to greatly exaggerate any childhood disease that you or Dean had contracted and that, many years ago, I even referred to your and Dean's annual cold as a "mild case of pneumonia." I was fully aware of that and told Dad that this was entirely different. I asked him if he was concerned about the test results and he said that he wasn't. He just thought that our doctor, whom we have known since both you and Dean were babies, was being cautious and doing the right thing with all these tests. Just as I was getting ready to ask Dad if he would please come with us on Monday, he said that he would take that morning off and I loved him more than ever for being so thoughtful and caring. We finally went to bed, but I couldn't sleep. Too many thoughts went through my head and none of them were pleasant or comforting.

When you had the MRI, you were wearing that blue, disposable, surgical cap and your head was strapped against the table. You didn't look like my eighteen-year old daughter, but more like the baby you were so many years ago. When I held you in my arms for the first time, I felt such pride and I silently promised you that I would love you, take care of you, and guide you and I was never going to let anything bad happen to you. Now, eighteen years later, I was thinking how easy it had been to keep the first three parts of that oath and I was praying that I would not let you down when it came to the "anything bad" part.

CHAPTER 31

❁

(Monday)

I am so afraid. I have to write something down, but I don't want to, because when I write the words down, they will stare me in the face and become a reality and I don't think I can handle it. Oh, fuck it all. I have to do it. I have cancer.

❀   ❀   ❀

Oh God, with Your infinite wisdom, please explain to me one day why it had to happen to our Sam, and please do this while I still have some faith.

CHAPTER 32

❁

(October/November)

I just read everything I wrote after we got the results of the tests. Didn't write it down very well. Think I was angry. I still am. However, tonight I want to write everything down again and I don't care how long it is going to take. Maybe my thoughts will be better organized than they were right after we got the horrible news. Writing always makes me feel better, or at least it used to. Whenever I had a problem or was ticked off about something or mad at somebody, I would write it all down in my diary. Then when I re-read it all, everything always seemed different and I felt less depressed or mad. Truthfully, I don't think that re-reading everything I am about to write down is going to make me feel any better. There are lots of things to talk about and I hope that I don't get things out of sequence, but I am not going to worry about it. It's really not all that big a deal.

Mom and I went to the hospital where I had all those tests taken. None of them hurt. They just took a long time and I didn't go to school that day. When we got home, I called Pam, and then I started studying for two tests. I never gave the hospital tests any more thought, because I was not worried about a thing. I asked Mom if she was dreading the results. She put her arms around me and said that she would feel a lot better after getting all the test results and find out that everything is all right. The rest of the week was fine and I did pretty good on the tests and the week-end was great.

Then Monday morning came. Had to go to our regular doctor, Dr. Gray, at ten, and he would have all the results. He's such a nice guy. Dean and I have known him since Jesus was a little baby. He was there and so were two other doctors. Turned out that one was an oncologist and the other was a neurologist, but we didn't know what kind of doctors they were until after Dr. Gray talked about the tests. He talked for the longest time, but he was not saying anything in particular and I was getting pretty damned impatient. Dad was listening very calmly, but Mom was squirming in her chair and I knew that she, too, was getting antsy. Then Dr. Gray said that Dr. Marshall, an oncologist, wanted to talk to us and when I heard what his specialty was, I got scared. Dr. Marshall said that I had a brain tumor. Dad and I just sat there, in shock. Mom said, "Oh God, you have got to be wrong." Dad was sitting between me and Mom and he was squeezing our hands so hard, our fingers turned purple. Dad asked a lot of questions, the biggest one being whether or not the growth could be surgically removed and then we found out that it is not an ordinary tumor. It is called "astrocytoma" and it is malignant. In short, it is cancer. When we heard that godawful word, Mom and I started crying right there in the doctor's office.

The doctors talked for a long time, but I cannot write it all down, because I don't remember all they said. The whole conversation seemed so unreal to me and I just knew that they were not talking about me, but about somebody else. Evidently, the kind of cancer I have can be treated with or without surgery, but even if you have the surgery, for some reason or other, the whole tumor cannot be removed. And also, since it is such a delicate operation, there might be a lot of side effects. I don't remember all of them, but he mentioned speech, thinking, memory and reasoning impairment, so the operation might result in an extremely shitty quality of life. The doctors recommended chemotherapy and radiation and Dr. Marshall said that these procedures have excellent results in many cases. I said a quick prayer, asking God to include me in the "many cases." It all sounded so bad and so very, very, scary, but none of it had sunk in yet. I kept having this feeling that it was not happening to me, but to another person in the room and I was wondering how Mom could possibly be so upset about this invisibility.

They talked for at least another thirty minutes, but I could and would no longer listen. I heard them talking, but nothing registered in my mind and I wanted them to answer my question that I had not asked yet, but they continued bull-shitting and I felt that everybody in the room knew what I wanted to ask, but they didn't want me to. When we left the office, Dr. Marshal shook hands with us. When he took my hand, I said, "Thank you", although I had no idea what I was thanking him for and then I asked him how many years I had left. Mom and Dad put their arm around me. The doctor told me that we should go home, sort out everything we had just heard and worry about my question later. I told him that I didn't want to worry about it later, I wanted to know now and I told him that I was not going to leave Dr. Gray's office until he told me the truth. I asked him a very simple question, but it took him forever to answer it. I think that he hated answering that question almost as much as I feared the response, because he took his sweet time. First he said that he was very confident that I would react positively to the treatments and that age, an important factor, was in my favor, and that my chances of leading a normal and rewarding life were excellent, and that there have even been cases where patients went into remission. I was beginning to get angry about him just beating around the bush, but then he gave me the answer. Why the hell did I have to ask? Why couldn't I have kept my big mouth shut? Why was I so anxious to find out that I only have a few years at the most? And why the hell did it have to happen to me?

I don't remember much about the drive home, except that I was sitting in the front with Dad and he was holding my hand. Mom was talking very calmly, but non-stop, about how she just knew that I was going to fool science and outlive everyone in the family. I also remember that Dad had to stop at a railroad track for the slowest-moving train in the history of the railroad and I was getting so damned irritated, because all I wanted to do was get home, although I had no idea what I wanted to do when I got there. Dad told us to try and be patient, because there was nothing any of us could do about it. Mom said there was something to do. She got out of the car and yelled, "Speed it up, fuckhead!". In spite of everything, Dad and I giggled and Mom said that we should try our best never to lose our sense of humor, no matter what the future has in store for us.

I called Pam as soon as I got home and she raced over and I had to tell her everything. Pam started crying, but strangely enough, I didn't. I had not seen Pam cry in ages. She said that we have been friends for many years and that she loves me and that she's going to try everything she can to help me and make things easier. I told Pam that I don't want to tell anyone in school yet.

Before I went for my first chemo treatment, I had to talk to the nurse at the oncology clinic. Her name is Brenda and she's nice. She does not believe in bull-shitting and she answers all your questions. She explained to me what I could expect. She said that it might make me feel tired and a little ill for a day, so she suggested that I get it done on Friday afternoon and then I'll have the whole week-end to recuperate. She said that she was sorry if that messed up my social life and I told her I was sorry that I didn't have one. I went that Friday for my first treatment and it took about forty-five minutes and it was not too great.

Don't feel like writing anymore. Pam called and asked me if I wanted to fart around with her for a couple of hours.

❦   ❦   ❦

Sam, I wish I could erase that day at the doctor's office from my memory, but I am afraid that it will stay with me for the rest of my life. Up to that day, our life had been easy, carefree, happy and full, and we had never been faced with any situation we couldn't handle. My main fear when it came to you and Dean had always been that one of you might get involved in a car accident, but the thought that either one of you might be diagnosed with an inoperable brain tumor had never entered my mind, and nothing in life had prepared us for it. I cannot describe how I felt that day in the doctor's office, besides numb, empty and lost. Dad later said that he felt like he had been hit in the groin with a baseball bat. The thought that you, our daughter, might not have a chance to live a full and happy life, had not yet sunk in.

As soon as Dad and I got home, the phone rang. It was Dean and his reaction to the terrible news, pure silence, was heart-breaking. Dad and I talked most of the night, about you, about what you must be going through, about how you were going to cope and what we could possibly do to help you.

The next evening, I tried to call Hank in Canada, but he was out of town. I didn't want to talk to Mona and she was a little irritated when I would not give her my reason for calling. Dad and I talked about having to tell his parents but neither one of us wanted to do it. I think that it was Wednesday when I called Grandma and I didn't give her any details, just the basic, cruel, facts. She was quiet for a few seconds and then said, "Well, of all the thoughtless things to do, Helen, waiting about two days before telling me about my granddaughter, tops the list." Sam, I did something I have been wanting to do for many years and I told her to shut up. It felt so good, I repeated it. Sam, it didn't slip out, it was deliberate.

A few days later there was a letter from Grandma, addressed to you. Since I had no earthly idea what she could have written and since I was afraid that the contents of the letter might possibly upset you, I decided to read it. I took the lampshade off one of the lamps and held the letter above the naked light bulb. It did not work and I thought how typical of Grandma to buy expensive envelopes instead of cheap, thin ones from K-mart, which make reading through them not much of a challenge. I boiled some water, held the envelope over the steam and it came open. The note was sweet and loving and I was ashamed of myself. No, I should have been, but I wasn't. I could not find any glue in the house to re-seal the envelope, but I found Dad's glue gun in his workshop and I succeeded in gluing the envelope to the workbench. It took the steam iron to get it free. Making the envelope look halfway decent was a chore and it required more ironing and a little spray starch. The end result was far from neat, but you didn't notice it. Sam, Honey, I swear that was the only letter I have ever opened.

All the medical books we checked out from the library or that we bought, all the pamphlets and brochures we could get our hands on and all the doctors we talked to over the next few weeks made me wish for two things: more faith in God and a simple mind. When Hank and I were little, our mother, the grandmother you never met but would have liked very much, took us to church sporadically. After she died we moved in with our grandparents, and going to church was no longer an option. We had to go every Sunday. Truthfully, just because one goes to church, doesn't necessarily mean that this person has faith or believes in God, at least that's my thought. I think quite a few skeptical people occupy church pews. Again, that's my thought. I always had faith and I always believed in God, but how easy it is to do that when you're happy, life is great, your blessings abundant, your worries few and your cup runneth over. It is not quite that easy to have much faith and to believe blindly in God when you're faced with a catastrophe, at least that's how I felt. The God I had always believed in until you became ill, was kind, knowledgeable, caring, down-to-earth, always forgiving, infinitely patient, a non-smoker and non-drinker, not very athletic, loving, with a terrific sense of humor and He always, without fail, had an answer for everything. I don't like to say this, but I lost a lot of faith after you were diagnosed with cancer and I was furious at God. I did not hold Him personally responsible for your tumor. I was convinced that the God I believed in was just as distressed and miserable about you being stricken with an incurable disease as we all were, but I just wanted a creditable explanation of why it had to happen to our eighteen-year-old daughter, and I did not get it. Our minister was a sweet, young man, who, no matter what the subject of his sermon was, always ended it with an example of one of God's many kind acts, and I got angry listening, because I didn't feel that God had been overly kind, at least not to you. I stopped going to church and did not go back until many months had passed and it took me even longer to make up with God and even longer than that for my cup to be half-full again. However, I continued to pray and I did this with a fervency that would have impressed the Pope and made any nun envious. What I basically prayed for was strength for you, Sam. Strength to accept this disastrous and fatal illness, strength to make each day meaningful in spite of the heavy yoke on your shoulders, strength to bear the pain and discomfort of this damned (Sorry, God) chemotherapy and the strength to eventually face the inevitable. Praying became a habit.

I also wished that I was simple minded, because I might be gullible, trusting and naive, and I might never doubt the words of those who possessed more wisdom, which would be just about everybody. All that was wishful thinking. I read every article and book on astrocytoma, this dreadful form of cancer, and Dad and I learned more about this monstrous condition than we cared to know. Those were the facts. Having simple and uncomplicated intellectual faculties might have made me susceptible to believe every optimistic word from well-meaning friends and doctors, but I did not and I could not. Allow me to use an old cliche, Sam. Whoever said that "A little knowledge is a dangerous thing," was full of you-know-what and he or she evidently never had a child with cancer. In my opinion, a little knowledge is not dangerous, but comforting. Acquiring too much enlightenment, insight and education, well, that's dangerous and petrifying.

CHAPTER 33

❀

(November again)

I got tired of writing last time, whenever that was, so I quit. The last thing I talked about was that I was so scared to lose my hair, but that hasn't happened yet. Thank you, God, for small favors.

Had chemo yesterday and it didn't bother me as much as the first time, when I got pretty sick. Now Brenda is putting something in the I.V. which keeps me from getting so nauseous. Mom came with me the first time. She just sat there, held my hand and looked at the same page in a magazine for forty-five minutes. Pam took me yesterday. She also held my hand and then she started dozing, and it was so great to have her there. She spent last night with me. I told her that she didn't have to, since I might not feel good or want to talk or whatever, but she didn't care. She said that we have shared a lot of laughter and good times and that good friends also go through hard times together. She's the best friend I've ever had. When I told Mom that Pam was spending the night, she just stared at me without blinking her eyes for a long time. Asked if she was all right and she said that her eyes were filled with tears and she was afraid that the slightest movement, such as the blinking of an eyelid, might set them free. When Pam came over, Mom gave her the biggest hug and told her she was a blessing. I haven't missed any school yet. With the exception of Pam and some other close friends, I haven't told anybody in school that I have cancer. I don't want the whole world to know about it and they'll find out soon enough when I start losing my hair. I don't want them to know, because they might feel sorry for me and I don't think I could handle their pity. Truthfully, I don't feel all that much different. I just get tired quite a lot. The only time I feel not real good is Friday evening, after chemo, but I am O.K. the next day again.

Pam and I didn't do much last night. She called Dean at his apartment and they talked for a while. I tried to watch the movie that Pam had brought, but I kept falling asleep. Pam told me the next morning that I had missed the juiciest R-rated movie ever, with the most explicit sex scenes that left nothing to the imagination. I had to laugh, because we've seen that movie at least three times and it doesn't even have any smooching in it.

Alan and I dated a little last summer, but we have not gone out at all since school started. I am glad about that, because I am not all that interested in dating at the moment. I am just wondering if Mom went to school and talked to my teachers. I am not going to ask her. Either she did or she didn't.

I am going to a cancer support group every Wednesday evening. At first I didn't want to go and I told Brenda, who had told me about it, that I didn't want to be around people who were on the verge of dying, but she urged me to attend, and I am glad I went. There were about twelve people at the first meeting, and I am the youngest one. I had to stand up, introduce myself and tell them why I was there. I had a slow start, but once I got going, it was very easy. A few of the people are in remission and they look pretty good and healthy and it gave me a lot of hope. One lady had a cancerous tumor removed from her lymph nodes and as soon as she found out that she was in remission, she celebrated by buying herself a bright-red sports car, that she drives too fast. She said that she could barely come up with the down payment and she has to take money out of her savings account to make the monthly payments, but she doesn't care. I get along real well with Mary, who is nice and honest. She had a breast removed and is still taking chemo. She showed me a picture of herself, taken before she got cancer. She had beautiful, long, blond hair. She lost it all and now she wears a wig and it looks pretty natural. She said that at first she was deeply depressed about losing all her hair and that's all she could think and talk about. Then she changed her whole attitude and outlook on life. She said that she was happy to be alive, bald or not, and she never knew how beautiful life was until she realized that it could be taken from her in a New York minute. She started enjoying little things in life, such as reading a good book, a hug, a nice glass of wine, a hot bath, things she had always done, but never appreciated. One of the others yelled, "What about a good screw, Mary?" and she said that she didn't mention that, because she had always liked that. She cannot understand how she ever got so upset about futilities, like getting a speeding ticket. She got one on the way to our meeting and she tore it up.

The word "death" is never mentioned at those meetings. No, I take that back. The subject was brought up one time, and everybody handled it about the same way. They said that everybody is going to die sooner or later, but they don't know when that will be and that we have a better indication of when that day may come than someone who does not have cancer.

I am also going to a counselor once a week, whose specialty is dealing with cancer patients. This was Mom's and Dad's idea. I didn't like the idea at first and I told Mom that I didn't want to talk to a middle-aged, bearded guy with horn-rimmed glasses. Mom said that she wanted me to go at least once, just to find out if he was indeed middle-aged, etc. I went and it was the best hour and the guy is fantastic. He is young and wears very tight jeans. He's trying to make me understand and see that I should enjoy the crap out of each day and not worry about what the next day may bring. Don't think he said "crap", but "enjoy life to the fullest". I am trying very hard to do that, but sometimes it's difficult.

Everything at home is very normal. Mom and Dad treat me the way they always have. The only difference I notice in Dean is that he now gives me a long hug when he gets home and another one when he goes back to college. He also talks to me a lot more.

Crying seems a waste of time and energy and I want to save both. I know that Mom cries and she hardly ever used to. She once proudly claimed to be the only woman in the theater who did not cry when Rhett Butler walked out on Scarlet. When Pam and I got to school one day last week, I remembered that I had left my book review for English at home. We were early, so Pam drove me home and I quickly ran inside. Yelled at Mom that I was home, but there was no answer. She was in the shower. I heard the water running and I could hear her crying and she was saying, "Oh God, why is life so damned unfair?" over and over. It scared me a little and I felt so sorry for Mom and all of a sudden it hit me big time that all I have been doing for the past weeks is think about myself and I really have not given Mom's and Dad's state of mind very much thought. Didn't want Mom to know that I had heard her. Kept thinking about her all during first and second period and decided to give her a call. The answering machine picked up and I left a message telling her I loved her.

When I get tired, I do feel sorry for myself to the point where I cannot think clearly, and once in a while, when I wake up in the middle of the night and cannot go back to sleep, I get depressed and I cannot wait for the night to be over. And sometimes, no matter how hard I try not to think about it, since I am supposed to live one day at a time, I cannot help but think about high school and going to college and then I wonder if I'll even make it to graduation next year. I want to help Pam write her valedictorian address. Most of the time I am happy though and then there's no doubt in my mind that I am not going to be one of the lucky ones and go into remission.

Pam is sure that she'll get a scholarship to Baylor and her dad has agreed to pay all her other expenses. Pam said that her mother is wondering why the S.O.B. has been so generous lately. She reckons that he feels guilty about something and she hopes that the feeling does not start wearing off for years. The phone just rang and it was Dean. He was fine and he wanted to talk to Dad about his insurance because he had just had a fender bender. When I asked him how much damage there really was to his truck, he said that he had just called a tow truck. Fender bender, my ass, major wreck, Dean. He asked to talk to Mom. I thought that Mom was going to be furious and give him a long lecture about defensive driving and all that shit, but no. She said, "Thank God you're all right. These things happen. I'll tell Dad to give you a call. Love you, Sweetheart." I don't recall her saying anything like that when I hit the "Handicap Parking Only" sign last year, and that was just a minor repair to the car.

I had to dropout of P.E. and am now taking a business class instead. It's the most boring class, but also the most fabulous, because John Griffin is taking it. He and I talk quite a bit now. What I really hated more than anything was that I cannot play basketball anymore. I had a long talk with Coach and I ended up in tears, which I hated, but she also cried, so my own tears didn't bother me all that much. She asked me if I wanted to help her with the coaching, but I cannot do it, at least not yet. I don't even want to go to the games anymore.

❧   ❧   ❧

Sam, it made me so happy to read that you thought that everything at home was normal and that Dad and I treated you like we always had. Right after you became ill, I started leading somewhat of a double life. The first one was meaningless and it started as soon as you went to school and I was left with eight hours to kill. No matter what I tried to undertake or concentrate on, my thoughts always went back to you and I never completed any task or project I had started. The only thing I accomplished was getting more and more depressed.

I considered the hour between 2:00 and 3:00 PM my "transition period." I would shower again, dress, and force myself into a better and more cheerful frame of mind.

Then, when you got home from school around three-thirty or so, my second life started. This was the important one, the life that really mattered, and I made every possible effort to act like the mother I had always been and I must have succeeded, or you would not have mentioned that things were normal at home.

Dad and I had never been very sociable. Occasionally we had friends over and we enjoyed being entertained from time to time. Early in November we received an invitation to a party, given by someone from Dad's office. Neither one of us wanted to go, but Dad said that the diversion might do us a world of good and it would take our mind off of you for a couple of hours, so we went. As soon as we entered our hosts' home, I recognized quite a few people and all I wanted to do was turn around and go home. Some of them asked how you were doing and I told them. Others consciously avoided the subject and that made me feel uncomfortable. I felt that Dad's and my presence was cramping their conversation. We left early. Looking back now, I don't think that any of the guests did or did not say anything that made me feel ill at ease. The naked truth was that I did it to myself. I think that I was envious of the other couples, not all of them, just those with healthy teen-age daughters. Although I did not wish for your disease to strike anybody's child, I am sure that the thought of why it had to be you and how come it had not happened to any of their daughters crossed my selfish mind. After that evening, Dad and I politely declined most invitations. My excuses were always lame. I should have been honest and tell whoever had invited us, that we were going through a difficult time and that we were unable to be around people and I know that everyone would have understood and accepted that. Sam, I think that I began to avoid people in general. I didn't even want to talk on the phone anymore and I let the answering machine pick up messages.

Sam, I just read over the above paragraphs and they sound deeply depressing. Don't get the wrong impression, please, by thinking that Dad's and my life was miserable and wretched, because it was not. However, it seemed that our mood was always a direct result of the way you felt. When you were feeling well and happy and cheerful, Dad and I felt close to exalted. When you had a bad day, we felt sad and discouraged. Do you know what really made our day, Sam? Listening to you and Pam talking and laughing and giggling. Such wonderful sounds.

I made an attempt to force my head to only absorb positive thoughts and I continued to have the same dreams and hopes for you. They included high school graduation, rooming with Pam in college, a four-year degree, a happy marriage and a dozen healthy babies. My mind was fully aware that there was a very good chance that all these hopes and dreams might not be materialized, but my heart could not accept it. I absolutely refused to think about life without you, because it might not be considered a life anymore, just a succession of bleak days. Dad was just as devastated about your disease as I was, but he handled it better and he was not quite as consumed with anger and frustration as I was. His work kept him busy and he was good about living one day at a time. Dean could not accept the fact that there was something wrong with his sister. Sometimes I felt so helpless and I didn't think that I was enough support for him. He didn't talk all that much to Dad about you and even less to me, but I do remember one incident. Dean called one morning before he went to class. He sounded so sad and lonely and I asked him if he would like to go out for lunch or an early dinner after classes. He said he'd like that, so I drove to Waco. When I got to his apartment, he was sitting outside on the steps. What I saw was not my handsome and mature son, but a little boy in dire need of a shave and a hug. We went out for barbeque, but he didn't eat or say much. He didn't start talking until we were on our way back to his place. He said that he had always known that life was pitifully short for a lot of people, but he just never thought or imagined that his sister would be one of them. He talked for a long time and then he started crying. The only thing worse than seeing the tears of your nineteen-year old son is listening to the quiet sobbing of your forty-one-year old husband. When he got out of the car, Sidney came up to him, put his arm around Dean and told him, "Hey man, good to see you." I thought how extremely fortunate we were to have a Sidney, Pam and Emma in our lives.

Sam, I am rambling on and I am not even sure if I am typing all my thoughts in a correct, chronological order. Bear with me, please, I'll get through it all. I mentioned earlier that Dad and I declined most invitations, but we did go to the open house given by the medical building that Dad's firm had designed. Dad was very proud of it, as he should be, and there was no way I was going to disappoint him by telling him that I was not interested in going. It was a semi-formal affair with a band and, since I didn't have the proper attire, Dad told me to go shopping for something appropriate. Emma came with me and she selected something that I would not have chosen myself. I told Emma that it might look good on Cher, but not on me, but Emma convinced me that it looked good on me and that she would not be able to find anything more appropriate for the occasion in a million years. As soon as we got to the party, I felt suffocated by all those people and I didn't know how I was going to make it through the evening. Dad was having the time of his life and did a lot of mingling. I got involved in a long conversation with one of the doctor's wives and I felt that I was doing admirably well keeping up my end of the conversation until she started talking about fashion. She asked me if I thought she was wearing the right accessories to go with her dress. I wanted to tell her that I had a very sick daughter at home and that I didn't give a flying fart what she was wearing and that I cared even less about her jewelry, which was very fugly, as Dean would say. She looked at me in a funny way and it dawned on me that maybe I had voiced my thoughts out loud instead of thinking them and it bothered me. The only thing I enjoyed about the evening was to see Dad happy and to feel his arms around me when we danced.

After the open house, I decided that it might be a good idea to seek some professional help for myself and I made an appointment with your counselor, Dwight Lucas. I knew very little about the man, except that he came highly recommended, charged a steep hourly fee, and liked snug-fitting clothes. As far as Dad and I were concerned, he could have charged three times his fee and wore tights just as long as the sessions were beneficial to you, which they were. Sam, don't worry, we didn't talk about you, but we discussed the way I treated you, about me being a little too over-protective at times, etc., all sorts of things that will not come as a surprise to you. Then he mentioned that I needed physical activity, which would make me tired and consequently sleep better at night and it might also do wonders for my mind. I took the word of this professional man, who looked barely older than Dean.

I took up yard-work with an ardent enthusiasm. Right after you went to school in the morning, I would piddle around the house for a while, shower, and get the mower out. Sam, please don't ask me why I showered before doing yard work. I have no idea myself. I mowed our huge yard Monday through Friday, and whether the grass needed it or not made absolutely no difference. After I finished mowing for the day, I would water the yard to keep the grass growing so I could mow again. I would stop around two in the afternoon, shower again and wait for you to get home from school. The yard started developing bald spots from all the attention I gave it. These places were fertilized and watered and as soon as the new grass started coming through, I would get the machine out again. I took it very personally when the grass became dormant late in the fall and there was nothing there to be cut. Emma said that the grass was not dormant. She said that the grass was disgusted with my obsession, because "Helen, you don't give the grass a friggin' chance. As soon as it starts growing you mow it down with that effing machine and I think it's beginning to take the defeatist attitude of 'Why in the hell should I bother to grow when all she does is come around with that shitty, noisy and smelly apparatus'?" I accepted Emma's explanation. I wasn't quite ready to give up mowing, so I asked some of our neighbors if they were interested in me doing some yard work for them. They were very nice, but totally disinterested in me stepping foot on their lawn. Mrs. Myers said, "Not in this lifetime, Helen," and I took that as a definite "No."

I decided to put mowing aside until the following spring and I began to spread top soil. I ordered it by the truck loads and I covered every square inch of yard, thereby suffocating the few blades of grass that had stubbornly survived all my previous attention. When I had raised the entire yard approximately two inches, it was time for me to undertake a different project. I looked around the yard, which looked pitiful, and decided to start trimming trees and bushes with a handsaw. Anything up to five feet from the ground was cut off and burned in a big barrel. This resulted in making the trees and bushes look absolutely ridiculous and the stink upset the neighbors and they started complaining a little, so this was a very short-lived project. Do you remember, Sam, when we had those high winds for a week and all the soil started blowing around the neighborhood and everybody complained, and rightfully so? Dad suggested that my next project could be washing everyone's windows. Dad was so sweet, though, and he supported all these insane and asinine projects of mine, because all that activity had a very positive effect on me. I felt better, less depressed and totally exhausted in the evening and I could now eat three scoops of ice cream without having to worry about what the calories were doing to my butt. Dad seemed so happy that I was doing better mentally and he decided that what was good for the goose might be good for the gander and he took up jogging. The first time he could barely make it around the block and he looked so bad when he got home. He couldn't catch his breath and you wanted to call EMS. He did just fine, though, and before long he was up to several miles a day. Sometimes, in the middle of the night when Dad woke up and knew that he couldn't go back to sleep, he would put on his jogging shorts and run until he felt better.

Sam, when you repeated my statement about me not shedding any tears during the epic saga *Gone With The Wind*, you were only partially correct. I did cry at the end of the movie when Rhett Butler left Scarlet standing there in the mist with her finger up her you-know-what, but only the first time I saw it. The second, third and fourth time I did not need a single tissue.

CHAPTER 34

❀

(Late November)

Thanksgiving is just a little over a week away and I am anticipating it with very mixed emotions. Mom asked me if I would enjoy having Pam and her family over and I said that would be great. Also, Grandma and Grandpa are coming, like they do every year and they're spending four nights with us. I told Mom that I wish they would just come for dinner and then leave, and Mom said that she's had that same wish for years. Dean is bringing Sidney home for Thanksgiving. He's a neat guy. Before Dean brought him home the first time, he told us that Sid was Jewish, so Mom rushed out and bought a Jewish cookbook. Then a few days later when she told Dean what she was planning on fixing, Dean laughed and told her that Sidney's favorite foods were pizza, hamburgers and pork chops. Mom decided that there was no need for "kosher" and she asked me to return the cookbook.

Dean told me the other day that it might be nice if the four of us, meaning him, Pam, Sid and I did something together on Thanksgiving and the day after. I told Dean that he should not feel obligated to include me in his plans and that they might have a better time without me and that Sid might not be too happy to be stuck with me. Dean got mad, really furious and he yelled, "Why cannot you just stop feeling sorry for yourself for one goddamn minute? If I didn't want to do anything with you, I wouldn't have asked you, you ungrateful, spoiled brat." Then he went to his room and slammed his door. I am sure that Mom and Dad heard every word, but they didn't say a word and Dad didn't even say anything about Dean saying "goddamn" which he hates. I was pretty upset and mad for a long time and yes, I did feel sorry for myself big time. How can I help it? I am beginning to lose some hair and that is so damned depressing. Mom keeps telling me that it is only a temporary loss and that it will start growing back when I stop taking chemo. When the hell is that going to be? Mom wanted me to go out with her and buy a wig for me, but I am not ready for that and when that time comes, I'd rather go with Mary from the support group. Her wigs are great-looking. Mom asked me if I remembered the perm she gave me a few years ago. Of course, Mom, how could I possibly have forgotten that? Anyway, she thinks that it may help my hairdo if I got a real curly perm. Have to think about that. Want to ask Brenda if all those solutions in the perm will make me lose more hair. If so, to hell with it.

I am getting sidetracked. I finally stopped feeling sorry for myself and I started thinking about Dean and what he must be going through and I started feeling a little ashamed of myself. I wanted to talk to him, but when I knocked on his door he told me to leave him alone. So I wrote him a note, telling him that I was sorry for acting like a supreme bitch and that I was looking forward to Thanksgiving and Friday and that I loved him. I put the note on his toilet seat. Dean never mentioned it, but when he went back to school, he gave me a longer-than-usual hug and told me to get together with Pam and think of things to do.

Let's see. How many people are we going to have over that long week-end. The four of us, Pam and her family, Sid and Grandma and Grandpa. That makes eleven. Maybe with that many at the table, Mom and Dad will do away with their annual, stupid, tradition. Every Thanksgiving, before we start dinner, Dad makes each one of say something for which we are thankful and that's just fine, except Mom goes on and on about the many things she is so grateful for and the meal is getting cold. Come to think of it, Thanksgiving would not be the same without it.

I am dreading Christmas with a passion and I wish we could just skip it this year. We always celebrate it in a big way and Mom and Dad go overboard with presents. It's also the only time that Mom and I bake, not just your ordinary baking, but from scratch. Usually, Mom already gets excited about Christmas in October, but she hasn't mentioned it at all this year. Maybe she's not looking forward to it either. I don't know why I am not. Think that sometimes I am afraid that it might be my last one. I'd better stop thinking about that and concentrate on one day at a time. Every year, Dean and I give Mom and Dad something from the two of us. I have been wracking my brain about what we can do this year, because I want it to be special. Maybe we can have our picture taken. I know Mom and Dad would like that. I just called Dean. He was studying and couldn't really talk, but he did like the idea and am going to set it up for Saturday. He's also getting his picture taken for Pam. Dean and I always exchange the usual gifts on Christmas, books and tapes, but this year I want to get him something to remember me by. That sounds morbid and I didn't mean it. Dean doesn't like jewelry. He wears a watch and that's about it. Maybe I'll get him a new one and have it engraved. Somehow or other I have to come up with some money before Christmas.

Pam and I were talking about what we wanted to do on Thanksgiving. We think it would be great to leave real early in the morning, drive to the coast, walk around the beach, have lunch, rent bicycles and then drive home. I asked Mom what time she would have Thanksgiving dinner ready and she said that was up to Emma, because she was going to do most of the cooking. I asked her if Grandma was going to help them, and Mom said not if she could help it. Pam's mother and Mom talked about it and they said we wouldn't have to eat until around seven, if that was all right with us. That way, we would have a long day. Just great with us. Pam and I haven't decided yet what we want to do on Friday. Guess I'll have to wait to see how tired I am going to be that day. Mom asked what we all wanted to eat on Friday, and Pam and I said meat loaf, if that was all right with Grandma, who is such a picky eater. Mom said that she didn't care what Grandma liked. Meat loaf was fine with her. She also said that she didn't think that Grandma was a finicky eater, but that she has the appetite of a Clydesdale horse. Emma is coming over again that day and Mom is really looking forward to it.

I am beginning to feel a little more cheerful about the holidays and it will be so much fun to have Pam and her family over two days in a row. I told Mom and Dad that I hoped Pam's mother would not say "mother fucker" in front of Grandma. Dad said that he could care less what Emma says and Mom is hoping for a tiny little "fuck" to slip out of Emma's mouth, just to see what kind of reaction it will get from Grandma. We couldn't stop laughing.

Am getting tired and I had better stop. Want to take a bath, do a little homework and go to bed. Sometimes it seems so useless to worry about homework when I feel that I may never make it to and through college and I wonder why I am knocking my brains out. Still, I want to graduate next year. That's all important to me and who knows what's going to happen. I am not ruling out remission and I am hanging on to that for dear life.

❧   ❧   ❧

Dad and I were not at all sure that we wanted his parents to spend the holidays with us. However, we had always asked them before and they had always accepted our invitation. We didn't want this Thanksgiving to be any different from previous years, so, of course, we ended up asking them. We had not seen them since Dean's graduation and since before you became ill and we didn't know how Grandma would react to you. You know how emotional she was. She could break out in tears at the drop of a hat or when something happened to one of her soap stars, but we didn't know how she would cope with reality, such as coming face to face with her granddaughter, who was beginning to lose a little weight and some hair. One night I drove Dad and myself crazy with all my worries about Grandma's visit, so the next morning I called her and I explained all my concerns to her. All she said was, "Helen, please give me some credit and don't tell me what I can or cannot say or do. I understand perfectly what Samantha and all of you are going through and I will not shed a tear, no matter how difficult that may be." I thought, "Touche, Helen" and told her that she could cry any time, just as long as it was not in front of you. They were flying in late on Wednesday. You went to bed early, because you wanted to feel rested the next day, and I stayed home waiting for Dean and Sidney, so Dad was on his own. He and his parents got home around ten. When Grandma walked through the door, she didn't give me her usual perfunctory, half-ass, hug. No, she walked up to me, put her arms around me and told me how deeply sorry she was about you and everything. I thought this was a big gesture on her part, so I refrained from asking if the "everything" referred to her having treated me so badly over the years. Dean and Sidney came right after Dad got home, but they only stayed for a few minutes and then drove to Pam's, and we all retired for the night.

The next morning, Thanksgiving day, I got up early and fixed breakfast for you, Pam, Dean and Sid and you were out of the house by eight. Then I fixed a big pot of coffee for Grandpa and Dad and they went to Dad's study with a bunch of newspapers, which they were going to read before watching football on TV. A few minutes later, Grandpa told me that the coffee was great, but that it would taste even better if he could put something in it. We didn't have anything and the liquor stores were closed, so I called Emma, who said that she had a plethora of good stuff and that she would be over just as soon as she dropped Joyce and Kim off at a friend's house. She said that she had been up since seven practicing her language for Grandma and when I asked her how it was going, she said, "fucking well." Emma came over around ten and she gave Grandpa a bottle of whatever and then she puts this unopened, liter bottle of tequila on the kitchen table. I asked her what she was planning to do with it and she said, "we, Helen, not me. I know that you don't drink very much, but today we are going to create the perfect margarita and you're going to love it." When I told her that I didn't think that margaritas would go with turkey, she said, "Helen, I see that you need educating. The beautiful thing about margaritas is that they go well with any meal, especially with turkey and dressing." Grandma came into the kitchen and wanted to know if we needed any help preparing the meal and Emma said that we had it all under control. Grandma went back to the living room and we put part 1 of *The Thorn Birds* in the VCR player and gave her a cup of coffee. Emma said that it was entirely too early to put that dead bird in the oven, but just the right time to fix some margaritas and we did. Emma wasn't happy with the first batch we made, but she said that it was a crying shame to pour it down the drain, so we drank it and we started on a new pitcher. Grandma kept walking into the kitchen and Emma said to me that it was hard to concentrate on what we were doing with her around, but she knew just what to do to keep Grandma out of our way. She fixed Grandma a margarita, which, she said, consisted of 2/3 of one thing and 1/3 of another. I told her that maybe 1/3 of liquor was too much for Loretta. Emma said that I was not catching on very fast and that it was 1/3 of mix. Emma gave it to her. Grandma took a long sip and said that it was the most delicious drink she had ever had in her life. Emma said there was more where that one came from and then we wondered how long it would take for Grandma to fall asleep. After about fifteen minutes, Emma said that she was getting tired of speaking like the Queen of England, and she went to see if Grandma was asleep yet. Now, get this, Sam. She tiptoed over to Grandma who had her eyes closed, stood right in front of her and whispered, "fuck, fuck, fuck."and since Grandma didn't say a word, we assumed that she was sound asleep. Emma visibly relaxed and then talked the way she always did. Sam, we laughed so much that day and it felt so good. I asked Emma one time if she thought you were doing all right and she said that you were in the best of hands and that we were not going to talk about you or Pam and Dean. Since neither Emma nor I were in any shape to pick up Emma's daughters later in the afternoon, we asked Dad and Grandpa. They were all footballed out and didn't mind.

Somehow or other, we managed to prepare Thanksgiving dinner and have it ready just before you all got home and we had the best time. All of you were talking excitedly about the day and there was so much noise at the table and a lot of friendly teasing and it was wonderful. Dad said grace, but didn't ask anyone to get up and say what they were thankful for and I only said how wonderful it was to share this special day with our loved ones. Sidney was a godsend and did a wonderful job keeping the conversations going, although Emma and I had a difficult time keeping up, due to the fact that our senses were somewhat dulled. Sam, you looked tired that night, but also so very happy. After we got the dishes done, Emma took her daughters home. She called us later in the evening. Said she didn't really have anything to talk about, except that she had been looking through a bartender's book and she found just the right drink to go with meat loaf. When Dad and I went to bed, I told him all the things Emma had done and said, and he couldn't stop laughing. The last sound I heard before falling asleep was Dad's chuckling.

Sam, I don't think you woke up until eleven the next day and you looked so very tired. Pam came over and the four of you wanted to do something, but you weren't up to it. Pam suggested to Dean that he and Sid go to the ranch for a couple of hours and she would stay with you. You told her that wasn't necessary, but she insisted. Pam was something else and saying that she was a loyal and caring friend is an understatement. Dad took Grandpa somewhere and Grandma and I did some laundry and piddled around the house until Emma came over. Emma and I didn't do much. Tried to watch a movie, but we kept dozing off. Grandma offered to fix the meat loaf, potatoes and everything else we had planned and Emma and I didn't hesitate and said "Yes, please" simultaneously. Yesterday we didn't want Grandma in the kitchen, today we didn't want her out of it. She was a good cook and she prepared a nice meal and she also baked several pies, some for that night and two for Dean and Sidney to take back to school.

That was absolutely the best Thanksgiving and I was so sorry when all the commotion was over. Dean and Sid went back to college on Sunday and I hated to see them leave. Dad and I took his parents to the airport and Grandma was actually nice when we got there. She thanked us profusely for our hospitality, told us to keep in touch often, wished us strength and said that we were doing a fantastic job with you, Sam. Then she initiated a big hug and told me to call her if I needed anything. Why did it have to take a major tragedy to make Grandma a little less callous and more human?

CHAPTER 35

❀

(December 1)

I did what little homework I had to do and then I took a bath and washed my hair. I literally screamed when I found a lot of hair in the tub and it took a long time to calm myself down. Mary and I went shopping for wigs last week and she helped me select two. One is almost shoulder-length and the other one is a little shorter. They both look good and you cannot tell that it's not my own hair. I don't need to wear a wig yet, but at least I have them when I feel I cannot go without one. I cannot have a perm. Wouldn't be good for my hair.

Dean came home with this beautifully wrapped box. When I opened it, there was a wig in it, not the kind that I bought last week, but a punk-rock one, kinda burnt-orange color with a stripe in it. It sounds horrible, but it looks better than the ones I bought with Mary. I put it on and asked Dad how he liked my new hairdo and he said that he didn't. Poor guy didn't even know it was a wig and thought that Mom had been messing with my hair. Dean said that he was getting tired of listening to me gripe about my hair and that's why he bought it. I couldn't find the right words to thank him, so I gave him a big hug and he told me he loved me. Since just about everybody in school knows by now that I have cancer, I am going to start wearing Dean's wig to school. Mom said it may just start a whole new trend.

I am still not looking forward to Christmas and wish it was already January. I am going to take a break and talk to Mom about it.

(Later)

I told Mom that she had not mentioned Christmas yet and I asked her if she felt the way I did about it. She was very honest and said that she was not looking forward to it all that much. She thought that Thanksgiving had been one of our happiest ever, at least what she remembered of it, and she has been thinking very hard what we could do for Christmas to make that day just as special as Thanksgiving had been. She asked me if there was anything in particular I would like to do. I didn't know what she was talking about, so I said, "Not really." Then she asked if there was some place I might like to visit. I was thinking Colorado or maybe even Mexico, but I decided I might as well go for it and I said, "Europe?". Mom thought for a minute and then she said, "Why not? Any country in particular?" Since I could only think of England and France, I mentioned those countries and Mom said those were wonderful choices. I was all excited. Couldn't stop asking questions. I asked Mom what she thought Dad would say, and she thinks that we'll have to work on him pretty hard, but that she's going to start tonight. Cannot wait for Dad to get home, so we can discuss it. Mom said that she'd rather talk to him alone first. Now I cannot think of anything else and I wish Dad would get home soon, so that Mom can talk to him and convince him about this trip.

❦   ❦   ❦

Sam, saying that I was not looking forward to Christmas all that much was not correct. I was dreading it with a passion. After Grandma and Grandpa left the Sunday after Thanksgiving and when Dad and I were on our way home from the airport I asked him if he could think of anything for us all to do for Christmas. He said that it was still about a month away and that he hadn't given it much thought yet. I often felt very optimistic about you, Sam, and many times I thought about you going into remission, lasting until age ninety. And then there were days when you looked so tired and you were quiet, almost lethargic, and you didn't feel like eating much and I then I had the horrible thought that maybe you would not be able to live your dreams and reach all your goals and I would look at your sweet face and fear that this might very well be your last Christmas with us, and that was such an unthinkable thought.

That evening I mentioned Europe to Dad and he didn't say "yes" or "no" right away, which was very encouraging, almost like a possible "yes". He said that Dean will be home on Saturday, which is only two days away, and that we should discuss it then. That sounded fair to me.

CHAPTER 36

❀

(Saturday afternoon)

I am so exited and happy and I feel so good. We're going to Europe for Christmas! I am too antsy to write. Pam is coming over in a little while and we're going to make a list of things to pack. I am so happy.

🍁   🍁   🍁

Sam, since Dean didn't have to go to work on Saturday, he came home Friday evening, which worked out very well. The four of us sat down and we talked for a long time about this overseas trip. Dad said that there was no way he could take two weeks off. Dean said that he wouldn't mind going to Europe at all, but that he'd rather stay home. I don't think he liked the prospect of not seeing Pam for two weeks. I told my family that the thought of me and you going, and leaving Dad and Dean to fend for themselves was not very pleasant, since we've always been together on holidays and that the four of us should come up with something different. Dad said that he and Dean would be just fine and that they didn't mind if just the two of us went. I always had the feeling that Dad and Dean had already discussed this, possibly on the phone before Dean came home. I asked you what you thought of that, Sam, and you said that was great, but still, you sounded a little disappointed. Dean went to see Pam and you went to your room and Dad and I talked for at least another hour about this trip. I mentioned to Dad that you had not sounded as enthusiastic and excited as I thought you might be and Dad agreed. Then he asked me how I would feel if Pam came on this trip with us and I started crying and told him that he had been reading my mind. I asked him if we could afford to pay for Pam's flight and he said that the money we had in savings for Dean's college education had not been touched, since he had a full four-year scholarship and that he couldn't think of a better way to spend some of it. I was thinking that no matter what my opinions of Grandma were, she had birthed a saint. We decided that it would be fair to ask Dean first what he thought of this idea, before we approached Emma. We waited for Dean to get home and we asked him. He said that the same thought had crossed his mind when he noticed that you had not sounded as excited as he thought you would be. He said that he didn't like the idea of not seeing or being with Pam for almost two weeks, but he said that they could talk to each other on the phone and that the time would go fast. He said that maybe he and Dad could do something nice for a few days. Dad gave him a big hug and I didn't know exactly what to say to him, except that he was a son to be so very proud of and that I loved him. I thought that I had something in common with Grandma by also having given birth to a saint. I called Emma to see if she was awake and she said that she was now. She said she'd fix some coffee and told us to come over. Dad stayed home, just I case you'd wake up, Sam, and Dean and I went to Emma and talked to her and Pam. No need to write that whole conversation down. Pam put her arms around Dean and said he was a keeper and that she'd miss him, especially Christmas day, but that you needed her more. Emma thought it was the best idea we could have come up with and she said that Dad was so generous and kind to do that. I told Emma that what we were doing seemed like a small token in comparison to all that she and Pam have done for us.

On the way home, I told Dean that I thought he should be the one to tell you the next morning and he did. He said later that you just about choked him with all your hugging and Dean said we had definitely made the right decision by inviting Pam.

CHAPTER 37

(December)

I cannot think of anything, except going to Europe. Have a hard time concentrating on homework, and I don't even care all that much about not caring more about it. Am I making sense?

Pam and I had our pictures taken and Dad is taking care of getting our passports and we were assured that we will receive them in time. Mom said that the best thing to do would be to find a very small apartment close to London. It's a lot less expensive than staying in a hotel and that way she can do the cooking. I am on a special diet to keep me from losing as little weight as possible and I have to be careful not to eat the wrong things. Dad, with the help of his secretary, Evelyn, found a small place about twenty miles from London. It only has one bedroom and Mom said that Pam and I can share it and she'll sleep on the sofa, assuming there is one.

Grandma called not too long after Dean told me that Pam was going with us. I told her that we were going to Europe for Christmas. Thought she might tell me how irresponsible we were to undertake such a big adventure by ourselves, without Dad and Dean, but she didn't. She thought it was a terrific idea. I told Mom that I had not given Grandma enough credit and she said that it might be a hereditary trait. A few days later, we received a letter from Grandma and Grandpa with a big check to cover some of our expenses. Mom and I couldn't believe their generosity and Mom called them immediately to thank them "profusely" as she called it. When Dad got home that evening, he seemed happy that his parents had been so nice and he was even happier about Mom already having called them. Mom doesn't really like to call Grandma and I don't blame her. I've listened in on some of their conversations and she's hateful to Mom. She was fairly decent to Mom when they were here for Thanksgiving, though, and Mom was nice in return and she even made Grandma laugh a couple of times, and that's no small accomplishment.

We talked to the doctor about my next chemo and he changed the date, so that I'll feel decent when we're overseas. He was sweet and he thought that the trip was a great idea and he asked me to send him a postcard, and I will. Dean and I had our picture taken for Mom and Dad for Christmas and it is pretty good, although I think that I look a little skinny. Dean and I wanted to buy a silver frame or it, but we couldn't afford it and we bought something else. His picture for Pam is great. Dean asked me if I thought Pam would like a gold necklace for Christmas and I told him that she would love it. He went out and bought something really pretty. He already wrapped it and asked me to give it to her Christmas morning.

Mom asked me a few days ago if I wanted to go shopping with her for Christmas presents for Dean and Dad, but I didn't want to go. Well, I wanted to go, but I was tired and I am trying to save as much energy as possible. Mom went by herself and bought some neat things for them. She also bought them a small, fake, Christmas tree, decorated it and put the presents under it. It looks real nice. Every Christmas we buy a real tree, but Mom didn't want to do that this year, because she was afraid that Dad and Dean wouldn't water it. Dad commented on how pretty the tree was. Don't think he even knows that it is not a real one. Mom said she'll tell him just so he won't put it by the trash can the day after Christmas.

❧   ❧   ❧

Sam, we only had a few weeks to make all the travel arrangements and it occupied all my free time, which was great. Emma and I did a lot of running around getting our trip organized and everything worked out well. I told Emma how wonderful it would be if she could come with us, but she said that she couldn't, because of Joyce and Kim. Maybe one of these days Emma and I can go on a nice vacation.

Sam, by this time you were beginning to lose a little weight, not too much, but it was beginning to show. Once in a while you might gain a few ounces back, but it did not equal the loss and it bothered me and Dad so much. When I hugged you, I could feel your bones beginning to protrude and I wanted to cry.

Sam, the picture of you and Dean is on the mantle in our bedroom and that's where it will always be. It is beautiful.

CHAPTER 38

(December)

Had chemo and it did not go over well and I still have a headache, but I don't want to mention it to Mom. I even had to miss a day of school, but I'd rather feel shitty now than when we are traveling, so I tried not to let it bother and upset me too much, but it did anyway. We are leaving in just about a week. I am not taking my diary with me, because we are going to be so busy and I won't have time to write.

Pam came over after school today and we talked a lot, like we always do. I started bitching about my hair, or rather the lack of it. It's beginning to look very puny and I should start wearing the wig Dean gave me more, but it itches and I feel better without it. Pam said that she knew just what to do and she ran out, drove to Walmart and came back with a lot of scarves. She put one on my head and Pam asked me if I liked the Aunt Jemima look, but I didn't. Then she tried something else and it looked good. Dean called when she was here. They are so sweet and nice to each other. I asked Pam if she thought they would ever get married and she said that the subject of marriage has not come up yet. I sure hope they get married one of these days. Oh God, do you think I will be around long enough to be maid of honor at my best friend's wedding? That would be so great and I promise I will not bitch (Sorry, God) about having to wear that friggin' (Sorry again, God) wig and scarf.

I talked to John Griffin today. No, I need to re-phrase that. John talked to me. I usually say "Hi" to him first, but this morning he started the conversation. He said that he saw Dean over the week-end and he told him all about our trip and he was happy for me and Pam. He also asked me to send him a postcard. I am sure I'll mail him several. I wonder how often he and Dean talk.

They were pretty good friends in high school, but I didn't know they still see each other from time to time.

Mom and I have been sorting out clothes and we put everything in the guest room and all we have to do now is pack it all the day before we leave. The other day when Pam was here, I told her that at least this year, we are spared from having to listen to "'Twas The Night Before Christmas". Mom heard me, because she yelled upstairs, "That's what you think. I already packed it." Anyway, when Dad saw what we were going to take with us, he almost flipped and said that the airline did not allow three suitcases per person, and he made us put a lot of things back. Pam has all her clothes ready. Her dad sent her spending money and a 35MM camera. All we talk about is the trip. I think that Mom is as excited as we are, but she hasn't mentioned the flight much. The only thing she has said is that she's not going to get out of her seat for the duration of the flight. Need to get busy and do some homework.

*   *   *

Sam, radiation and chemo were a vital part of your treatment and Dad and I dreaded those days, because we never knew how you were going to react. You often looked so worn-out and Dad and I were often at a loss of what to do and it made us feel helpless and inadequate. And then there were the times you had to go to the hospital for an MRI to check the tumor and waiting for the result seemed to take an eternity. I had several reservations about the trip and I discussed them with one of your doctors. He was so nice and helpful and he gave us the name of a physician in London whom we can contact, if necessary. I also hated to leave Dad and Dean, especially Dad, for two weeks.

You know, Sam, that I often bothered you with questions about Dean and Pam and I even had the gall to ask you one time if you thought they might be sleeping together. I don't know why all of that was so important. Either they did or they didn't and there was not a thing I could do about it. I asked Dad about it once and he said that he trusted Dean and Pam implicitly and that he didn't think there had been any sex between them yet. After Dad made that remark, I decided right there and then that it was useless to continue that discussion. I also trusted Dean and Pam implicitly, but I had very little faith in their hormones. Well, around this time of year they had been dating steadily for many months. Pam was very mature for her age, Dean was no longer a boy, but a man, and they were happy together and good to and for each other and who cares if they slept together. Emma told that she was not in the least concerned about them, because after Dean and Pam had been dating for a few weeks, she gave Dean a shoe box filled with condoms. Emma said that if they had sex on an average of three times a week, Dean wouldn't have to buy any more until age 86. Sam, I do think that the subject of marriage had already been brought up, but Pam didn't want to mention it to you, because she was so afraid that you'd never have a chance of being her maid of honor at her wedding.

No, for once the prospect of a long flight did not scare me very much. Being involved in a plane crash used to be one of my fears, but it didn't seem all that bad anymore. Not nearly as devastating as having a daughter with a brain tumor.

CHAPTER 39

❀

(January)

We got back from Europe a week ago and it was absolutely the most wonderful trip ever.

We went everywhere by train, had a lot of rain and some snow, saw everything we wanted to see, took a lot of pictures, saw "Phantom of the Opera" in the theater, which was awesome and bought a lot of crap. I was exhausted when we arrived at the apartment, so we didn't do much that day. The apartment, or "flat" as they call it over there, was all right. Pam and I shared a small bedroom and Mom slept on a pull-out bed in the living room, which was tiny. In spite of the fact that I felt tired a lot, we did just about everything that Pam and I had read about. Pam and I stayed in the apartment one day when I didn't feel well and Mom had the day to herself. Pam called Dean. I started writing John Griffin a postcard, but I couldn't get everything I wanted to tell him on one card, and I ended up sending him five postcards. Hope they all get there on the same day. Mom said that she was going to do some shopping for Emma. She said that she would be back by three, but didn't make it until about two hours later. She got on the wrong trains, even though Pam had told her exactly which ones to take. She also bought some candles and a tiny ceramic Christmas tree and some little presents for me and Pam to put under the tree. She called Dad almost every other day and Pam's mother twice. Mom did real well fixing meals and Pam cooked a few evenings. We had such a terrific time and everything was so nice and sometimes unreal and I didn't really want to go home and face chemo and school and whatever, but I missed Dad and Dean and some of my friends in school.

Dad, Dean and Emma picked us up at the airport and they were so happy to see us. Dad hugged me and said he was so happy to have us all home safely. Dean gave me and Mom a quick hug before he squeezed Pam for the longest time. Dean dropped us off and he took Emma home and then he and Pam went out for a few hours.

When we got home, Dad said that he and Dean had a surprise for me and that it was upstairs, and there, in a big box, was the tiniest puppy I had ever seen. She is light-colored and she's cuddly and sweet and I love her. I named her "Hope" and Mom and Dad said that was a nice and very suitable name. We put newspapers on the bathroom floor, but she either eats or tears them up and then she tinkles or poops on the bathroom mat. Before I go to school, I put her in the laundry room where we made a cozy corner for her. I put a blanket and some toys in her box in my room. Mom wanted her to sleep in the box instead of on my bed, but as soon as I put Hope in the box at night, she starts crying, so, of course, I pick her up, put her in bed with me and she falls asleep almost immediately. Hope also cannot be on the furniture, but yesterday, when I got home from school, Mom was sound asleep on the sofa with her arms around Hope, who was snoring a little. When Mom woke up, she said, "Don't say anything, Sam. Hope doesn't like the laundry room and I took the box out of your room, because she's not real fond of that either." I asked Mom if Hope spends any time in the laundry room and she said, "Oh yes, about a minute each morning. I pick her up right after you leave for school." I am tired and I am going to take a nap with Hope.

❦   ❦   ❦

That trip was a godsend and it did wonders for you. The fact that Pam shared it all with you made the vacation even more meaningful. It was enjoyable to be a tourist in a foreign country and to see so many places of interest that I had only read or heard about. What made the trip so special for me was seeing you so relaxed and happy, hearing your frequent laughter and listening to you and Pam giggling in bed, and just being with you.

About Hope. Dean found her on the ranch. He felt sorry for this stray puppy, took her home and he and Dad bathed her. He asked Dad if he thought you would like her and Dad thought you would be thrilled. Dad was wise and called the doctor to find out if you could be around a puppy and the doctor had no objections. Dad took her to a vet, who gave her all the necessary shots and he thought that this malnourished little thing was about ten weeks old.

When Dad asked him what kind of breed it was, the vet shrugged his shoulders and said, "Beats me." When I first saw Hope, I thought she was the most homely and ungodly-looking mutt I had ever seen, with her long legs, big paws, skinny face with long ears and she was cross-eyed. Then you picked her up and she put her front paws on your cheeks and she licked your face and you laughed and hugged her and looked so happy, and I thought that I had never seen a more beautiful and precious little animal. Dad was very adamant and told you that she should be paper-trained, because he would not allow tinkling and doodling in the house. We had no control over Hope's very active bowels and urinary system and she went whenever and wherever she pleased and then looked proudly up at us. Sam, I don't think that Dad cared a whole lot. We were thrilled that Hope made you so happy and we all got used to the smell of "Nature's Miracle" that we bought by the gallon. A little tinkle and doodle seemed very inconsequential compared to the look in your eyes when you held Hope. It took Hope quite a long time to do all her duties outside.

CHAPTER 40

❀

(March)

I haven't written anything important in weeks, for the simple reason that not much is going on. Also, I haven't felt all that well lately. I get so damned tired and sometimes I forget ordinary things and my mind is a blank and it scares me. I talked about it with Mr. Lucas and also with Brenda and they both told me that it might be a result of all the medication I am taking. They also told me to write things down. I tried that, but sometimes I forget where I put the damned notepad and I want to scream. This is what it must feel like to have the onset of Alzheimer's and it is terrible. The doctor told me not to worry about it too much. Well, that's easy for him to say. Sometimes when I am in school, I forget where I am and I want to cry, and then when I finally realize where I am I wonder why I am there and why it is so important that I graduate this year. I am going to do it. The doctor changed my medication, so maybe I'll start feeling better, hopefully very soon.

Today I feel pretty good, but I am still a little depressed after the dream I had last night. It was not really a dream, but more like a nightmare and the worst part of it was that it seemed all so real. I dreamt that I had died and I was lying in church in a godawful looking dress that Grandma had made. I tried to tell Mom to take that fugly dress off me, but I couldn't get the words out. Then this lady, who looked like Mrs. Cain, my clarinet teacher, started playing the organ and it sounded horrible and I wanted to yell and tell her to stop playing. I must have yelled, because the next thing I know is Mom holding me and telling me to wake up. I told Mom about the dream and she sat with me until I felt calm again and when she left my room she reassured me that she would never allow me to wear a sucky dress, especially not one made by Grandma.

It all made me think. I have done well about living one day at a time and not looking past tomorrow, but once in a while, when I feel rotten I cannot help myself and I think about the fact that I may not be around for as long as I would like to be. Mom and I have never discussed the arrangements for when "it" finally happens and I want to have some say in the matter, since it concerns me and only me. Mom, I am putting some clothes on the top shelf in my closet and that is what I want to wear when my time comes. I also want to wear the gold bracelet that you and Dad gave me for my sixteenth birthday and Dean's old leather jacket, the one with the patches. Mom, in my opinion, organ music sucks badly. I put two tapes on top of the clothes and please let them play that music in church. Pam will tell you which songs to choose. Don't worry, it's not hard rock. I just re-read this last paragraph and it sound so final and I cried, but it is a relief to get it written down. But what was I thinking? Mom is not going to read all my diaries for a long time. I'll write everything down again and give it to Pam and let her take care of everything.

❧   ❧   ❧

Sweetheart, everything was taken care of, just the way you wanted, down to Bette Midler singing "Wind Beneath My Wings".

CHAPTER 41

❀

(April)

This morning, when I woke up, I was in the absolute worst of moods and I told Mom I was staying home. She asked me if I was feeling all right. I was, but I just didn't feel like going to school. She made me get dressed and eat a little breakfast and then drove me to school. Pam always picks me up, but I called her and told her I wasn't going to be ready in time this morning. Mom said that if things didn't improve to call me and she'd pick me up. Things greatly improved and Mom, thanks for urging me to go to classes today.

After fourth period I had to go to my locker to get my assignment for government, which I finished a few days ago, but I couldn't find it and got all frustrated. I couldn't tell my teacher that Hope had eaten it, because I think I already used that excuse once, but I didn't know if it was for English or government. Whatever. I was turning my messy locker inside and out and a lot of crap fell on the floor. So I bent down and started picking things up and then I hear this voice behind me saying, "Hey Sam, let me help you with that." and there is John Griffin. We talked and then he asked me what I was doing Friday evening and when I said "nothing", he asked me if I would like to go to a movie with him. Would I? It's something I have been dreaming about. I told him that I would love to go and he said he'd call me later and then we could decide on a movie. I told Pam and she was so happy for me. John called that evening. He's going to pick me up at seven on Friday and then we're going to see a new release with Bruce Willis. I could care less what we're going to see, I am just so happy he has asked me. Friday is three nights away, three very long nights. I asked Mom if I could wear that new blouse of hers, the one she bought a couple of weeks ago. She said that I could, if I could find it. I must have worn it before, because it was in my closet with some stains on it. Mom said she'd take care of it. I am in hog heaven, I am so happy.

❀   ❀   ❀

Oh Sam, I have a confession to make and it is not going to be easy for me. I did something very humiliating and I was not proud of it and Dad was not happy with me. When I approached Dad about this subject that I am so reluctant to talk about, I told him that I was going to do something and that he was most likely not going to agree with it, but that I was going to do it regardless. What did I do? Here it goes, and please forgive me. Sam, I was not stupid and I was fully aware of the fact that you had your eye on John for the longest time. I also knew that nothing would make you happier than going out with him. Sam, I know I am not getting to the point, but I'll get there shortly, like now. Sam, I asked Frances Griffin, John's mother to have coffee with me. I knew Frances from PTA meetings and track meets. I also knew her from little league baseball and soccer games, where we would sit together on the bleachers under all sorts of weather conditions. O.K. Sam, I know you don't care about the weather, so let me continue. Neither one of us could comprehend why we subjected our sons to participating in a sport in which neither one showed much interest. Truthfully, Dean and John spent almost as much time on the bleachers as we did. Sorry Sam, you probably weren't interested in that little bit of information, either, and I cannot blame you.

I met Frances for coffee and I asked her to let me talk. I told her that you were doing as well as could be expected, which was not too great at times, that you were coping admirably well under horrible circumstances, but that I was afraid and so very, very scared that your dreams would never materialize and that, before you left us, it would be so great if one of your smaller dreams could come true, and that was having a date with her son on whom you had had a crush for years. There, Sam, it's all written down now and I feel a little relieved. Frances was nice and very understanding. The first thing she said was that John liked you and often talked about you. Sam, I don't know if that was true or if she only said it to make me feel better, but I loved her for saying it. She said that she didn't think that my request was all that strange and that she would do the same if she were in my position. She was going to talk to John that evening and, even if things did not work out, you would never know about it.

Sam, John showed up a little early that evening and you weren't ready yet. I was glad, because that gave me a chance to give him a hug. I cried after the two of you left and I told Dad that I was not proud of what I had done, but I just wanted you to have a little happiness and know what it felt like to go out on a date with someone you think the world of. Sam, I will never be sorry about what I did.

CHAPTER 42

(May)

Haven't written much lately. Went to the doctor yesterday to have some sores in my mouth checked. Losing my hair and some weight is one thing, but these painful sores are worse and I hate them. He gave me some medication and I hope it makes them disappear. It is Thursday evening and I have no homework. I feel like writing in my diary, which I haven't done very often lately. I want to talk about John, my first love. I hate to be too realistic, but he's probably also my last love. John and I went to the movies that Friday evening and it was the best evening of my life. He didn't hold my hand, but our arms touched on the arm rest between the seats and that was such a nice feeling. After the movie he dropped me off at home and said "See you later, Sam," and I hoped that later was very soon. He called the next day and asked me if I would like to watch a movie at his house that evening and I felt so happy I could hardly breathe. His mother, who is really cool, fixed spaghetti and we ate that on the couch while we were watching the movie. It was another great evening. When John took me home that evening, he asked me if he could start picking me up in the mornings and I told him that I would love it. Told Pam that John was picking me up from now on and she thought that was great and "great" is an understatement. We also go out on Friday evenings and I live for those nights. It took me a while to get up enough courage to ask him why he wanted to go out with me, out of all people, when he could have his pick of any girl in school. He said that he has always liked me but that he was afraid to ask me out because of him not being as smart as I am. I've always known that he's not the brightest, but I've never cared about that. His dad insists on him going to college after he graduates, but his mother wants him to do whatever makes him happy and that is going in the Air Force. John talked to Dad the other night about his plans. Dad told him that college is not for everybody and that making a career in the air force sounded like a good idea to him. John thinks that Dad is great and he is. A few weeks ago, John and I went over to one of his friends' house to watch a movie and hang out. After a while I started feeling sick to my stomach and I asked John to take me home and he did. Mom and Dad weren't home. Think they went to a movie. John put me on the couch and gave me my medication. I put my head on his lap and he covered us up with a blanket and then he gave me a little kiss on my cheek (first time he's done that) and told me to relax and go to sleep. Well, after that tiny kiss, I couldn't go to sleep right away. John did. When I woke up the next morning, Mom was still asleep and Dad and John were fixing breakfast and it smelled so good and I ate more than I usually do. After John left, Dad said that John was a very special guy. The best and sweetest thing about John is that I don't have to pretend to be someone else. He doesn't act upset when I don't feel well and screw up his evening. He is gorgeous and I love him and now I know how Pam feels when she talks about Dean. The other night John just dropped by and asked me to go to Lake Travis. Mom was just getting dinner ready and she fixed us a huge picnic basket. Then John's car wouldn't start and Mom let him take hers, which surprised the shit out of me because she doesn't even let Dad drive it. Dad told John that he would take a look at his car after we left.

When we got to the lake, we found this nice spot to sit down and we had the best time talking and eating and watching Hope swim in the lake. John said that Mom had packed enough food to feed an army, but he managed to eat most of it. After we finished eating, John said that he wanted to ask me something very important. He got down on one knee, took my hand and said, "Samantha Evers, would you do me the honor of going to the prom with me?" I just sat there, didn't know what to say, but did what I have dreamed about doing for so long. I put my arms around him, told him that I had loved him for years and that going to the prom with him was a dream come true. He told me that I was the best thing that had ever happened to him and that he loved me and then he put his arms around me and gave me a real kiss. It was the greatest, but it also scared me. John and I talked for a long time and I told him that I didn't think I was doing very well and that I might never make it to college and that sometimes, when I thought about not being here for much longer, I felt so scared and lonely. John never said a word. He put his arms around me, held me for the longest time and said that we were gong to make the best of each day. I love him.

We got home late, but Mom was still up. John told her that he had asked me to go to the prom. Mom looked so happy, but she didn't say anything. All she did was put her arms around John and told him that he was a godsend and a blessing. Dad still had to do some work on John's car, so she let him take hers home.

❧   ❧   ❧

Yes, Dad and I did go to the movies that evening. When we got home, you were both sound asleep on the couch. Dad covered the two of you up with another blanket and I called Frances. Wanted to tell her exactly what I thought had happened, but I was tired and not thinking straight and I ended up telling her that you were sleeping together. She just laughed and said she'd see John in the morning and suggested that we have lunch next week.

Sam, after reading all your above thoughts, I once again thought that I had made the right decision by talking to Frances. Sam, John genuinely liked and loved you. All I wanted was for you to have some nice dates with this unusual, sensitive and wonderful young man. When you came home that evening after going to the lake and after John left, you were so excited and I had not seen you that happy in a long time and I felt a little hope and I prayed that you would feel well the night of the prom and that it would be the most memorable night of your young life.

CHAPTER 43

❀

(May again)

Screw school. Don't want to talk, think or write about it. Mom and I went out and bought a prom dress. Since I am beginning to lose more weight, we didn't go for anything with bare arms and a low neckline. Took us a long time to find something pretty, but I told Mom that it was too expensive and that I didn't mind shopping a little longer. Mom said that the dress was just perfect for me and that the senior prom only comes once in a lifetime and that she didn't mind using Dad's credit card. I tried on the dress again last night and it looked loose. We only bought it a week or so ago and I am afraid I have lost another pound or so. Mom does not want me to weigh myself anymore and she threw the scales in the trash can. She said that she'd be happy to get the sewing machine out and make some alterations, but I begged her not to, because she'd probably ruin it. Pam came over, got some thread out, made a few adjustments and now it looks just fine. The prom is a week from tomorrow and I hope the dress will still fit. I am going to wear my short wig that night and a scarf over it that matches my dress. I complained to Pam that I look so damned pale all the time and she said that she'd be over early that Saturday and help me with some make up. John is going to wear a grey tux and I cannot wait to see him in it. Pam has a beautiful dress and Dean is wearing a black tux.

Last week-end when John was at the house for dinner, Dean came home and he asked John and me if we'd like to have dinner with him and Pam that evening and we both liked the idea. John is picking me up at seven and then we're meeting Dean and Pam in a restaurant before going to the prom at the convention center. I am feeling fairly well at the moment, but I don't know about a week from now, and it is a safe feeling that Pam and Dean are also going to be there.

Dad was in Dallas for a few nights last week and one evening Mom and I checked out a movie and we watched it in her bed, and Hope went sound asleep on Dad's pillow. It was a crummy movie and we turned it off after half an hour or so. Mom suggested that we go to sleep, but I didn't feel like it at all and I told Mom that it was time that we had a long talk together. She fixed us some tea and came back to bed. I brought up the subject of "death" which we have been avoiding for months and I asked Mom if she realized that I was not going to be around much longer. She turned out the light, put her arms around me and talked for a long time. She talked about being a mother and how painful and unfair it is to know that your own child may not outlive you and about how she wished that she could take my place because she has already lived a full life. And also, she will never understand why it had to happen to me and about how much she and Dad love me. She said that she hoped that Dad and I had given me enough love over the years to last me forever and that all the loving memories she, Dad and Dean have of me will keep them from going insane when I am no longer with them. We both cried a lot, but I think they were mostly tears of relief. Then Hope woke up and she tinkled on the bed-spread and Mom pretended to be mad and told her she was a bad puppy and Hope licked her face and Mom kissed her nose. Mom said that she doesn't think a dog trainer would be very impressed with the way we treat Hope.

❧   ❧   ❧

Sam, I had been dreading that talk for quite a while. There never seemed to be a good time to bring up death, but it had to be done and I think it made us both feel better. After you were diagnosed with a brain tumor, I prayed for the tumor to disappear. It didn't, although it shrank. I prayed for you to go into remission, but that was not to be. I prayed for you to be free of pain and, thanks to modern medicine, you never had any excruciating pain. I prayed that I didn't overwhelm God with my many requests for you. I prayed that, when the dreaded moment came, you would feel that all of us who love you so much were right there with you and that you were not alone. Oh God, please help us all.

CHAPTER 44

❀

(End of May)

I am so tired and I am not feeling all that great. Just want to write down that the prom was last night and that it was the happiest evening of my life. I love John so much and I wish I could live a little longer and spend all my time with him, but I don't believe that's going to happen. Hope just jumped on my lap and we're going to take a nap.

🍁   🍁   🍁

Pam came over around six the evening of the prom and she put some makeup on you and helped you get dressed. You looked so pretty and sweet that night, but also so fragile and vulnerable and so very thin. John came over an hour later. He gave you the biggest hug and a corsage. Then he pulled this little box out of his pocket and gave it to you with all his love and when you saw what was in the box, a little gold necklace with a heart pendent, your face lit up and you blushed when he fastened it around your neck. Then you left with your arms around each other and Dad and I knew that you were in good hands and we were so happy that you had slept and rested most of the day and were feeling as well as could be expected that night. Dad said he'd fix us some coffee. Seemed to take him an awfully long time, so I went to check on him. He was sitting at the kitchen table with his head in his hands, sobbing his heart out and I wanted to console and help him, but I couldn't. I just cried with him and we talked about how we were ever going to make it through life without hearing your voice, your laughter and your incessant talking. How we were ever going to make it without you, our precious daughter, our child.

Next to the Christmas picture of you and Dean is a framed photograph of you, John, Pam and Dean, taken at the prom. Dad and I wouldn't trade them for all the Van Goghs and Rembrandts in the world.

CHAPTER 45

❀

(June)

I made it. I did it. I graduated from high school. That was one of my goals. Think it may have been my last one.

❀　　　❀　　　❀

Grandma and Grandpa and Hank and his family and several of our friends came to your graduation. Emma's ex-husband came by himself and he, Emma and their two daughters sat behind us. Pam started her valedictorian address by saying, "Faculty, students, parents, loved ones and my dearest friend, Sam..." and I started crying, but I was not the only one. Sam, her speech was unbelievable, wasn't it, just like she is. Sam, when they called out your name and you walked across the stage with the help of John and accepted your diploma, your entire graduation class rose and cheered. Grandma had spent the entire day in the kitchen and had prepared all sorts of hors d'oeuvres for anyone who wanted to come over for a few minutes after graduation. Don't know how many showed up, but it felt that all your classmates were here at one time or another. I looked around for you, but couldn't find you. I went upstairs and there you were, already in bed, fast asleep, with your arm around Hope and your hand in John's. Felt this huge lump in my throat and it wouldn't go away, no matter how much I swallowed. I kissed the three of you and went downstairs again.

Sam, Dad took a whole roll of pictures at graduation, but none of them turned out. It's just extremely difficult to focus a camera when your eyes are filled with tears.

CHAPTER 46

❀

(July)

I am not doing well and I cannot write anymore. Dad gave me a tape recorder and a bunch of tapes and that's why I am talking into this machine. After graduation I could barely make it up the stairs. Dad, Dean and Mom took a lot of stuff out of Dad's study and made room for my bed and they took a lot of other things out of my room. Now I don't have to go up and down the stairs, and that helps.

I had a bad night last night. I heard Mom in the kitchen around three. Guess she couldn't sleep either. A little while later she asked me if I was asleep and I told her that I wasn't. She crawled in bed, put her arm around me and Hope, and whispered that she loved me over and over again. She used to do that when I was little and not feeling well and it felt good and safe and I finally fell asleep.

I had a really good day last week and I had a talk with Dad. I told him that I could not have asked for a better father and that I loved him and that I was going to miss him so much. Then I made a tape for Dean, one for Pam and a very long one for John, thanking them for all the things they have done for me and for all the love they have given me. Also made a short tape for Grandma and Grandpa. Emma came over this afternoon and she sat with me for a while and I thanked her for always being so nice to me and she put her head on my pillow and said, "I am going to miss you so much, you little shit" and then she cried. Strangely enough, I didn't cry. I just felt empty and sad.

Mom, one of these days you are going to read my diaries and listen to the tapes. I don't know when that will be. I often wrote down pretty bad things about you and I criticized you. Mom, that's the way I felt at the time. Just don't ever forget that, in spite of what I may have written, I love you with all my heart and I thank you for being there for me and for always loving me. Mom, if I didn't love you so much, I would have destroyed all my diaries.

John will be here in a few minutes. He comes every day. I am not up to going out anymore. When I am too tired, he just sits next to my bed, holds my hand and reads a book. He said the other day that we're just like an old couple. How I wish that could be true. God, I am pretty sure I'll see you very soon.

❋   ❋   ❋

I don't know exactly when you made this last tape, but I am pretty sure it was about a week before you died. Dad, Dean, Pam, Emma, John and I only left your side to take a quick shower and to change clothes. When the end came very near, Dean, Pam, John and Emma left the room. Dad and I held you. We kissed your sweet face and told you how much we loved you. You smiled and slipped away. Oh God, Sam, you were so young. Emma came into the room a few minutes later. She gave you a hug and, with tears running down her cheeks, said, "Katie, bar the doors. Here she comes, God. She's a handful."

God, this is for Your eyes only. You know what's in my heart and on my mind, so it should come as no surprise that my overall opinion of You was, at times, at an all time low. I will never understand why it had to happen to our Sam. She was too young, God. She had her whole life ahead of her. You never gave me a plausible explanation as to why you chose her. Maybe you didn't want to, because you knew that I would never have accepted it. However, I would like to thank you for so many special people, because without them, life would have been more than grim, it would have been unbearable. Thank you for Emma, this dear, loyal and loving friend with her wonderful sense of humor. She always managed to put a smile on our faces, or lift our spirits with an outrageous remark or a highly exaggerated story. And thank you for her daughter, Pam. I never realized how much I loved her until Sam became ill. Pam put herself in second place and concentrated all her efforts on making her friend's life easier and she did this so lovingly and selflessly. And bless John. Thanks to him and his wonderful ways, Sam experienced what it felt like to be in love and to be loved in return. Brian and I thought John was a gift from heaven. And thank you also for Sam's teachers and her friends, who were all so supportive and understanding. Please bless them all, God. And thank you most of all for answering one of my daily prayers, the one about giving Sam strength to eventually face the inevitable. She did that so well. I hope you were patient with her God. Emma was right. Sam could be a handful and I hope that you carried her in the palm of your hand until she got used to the routine.

Sam, Honey, at the beginning of this project, I wrote that I would like to give Dad a copy one of these days. I hope you don't mind, but I'd also like to give one to Emma and Dean. Wish I could send one to Grandma and Grandpa, but, for obvious reasons, that would not be a good idea. It is too bad, because I would like for them, especially for Grandma, to learn more about their only granddaughter and her family.

Sam, that's it. Aren't you proud of me for having started and finished a project? Thanks for not getting rid of all your diaries and the tapes and for trusting me to read them.

EPILOGUE

❀

My dearest Sam,

I waited three years before I started reading your diaries and it took me a month to type this journal. Much has happened in those years and I would like to tell you about it.

The first year was difficult, and, at times, we didn't think we could make it and we would happily have gone through all of the 365 days without a single birthday, anniversary or a holiday, because those were the hardest. Dad's hair turned completely grey and I acquired a lot of wrinkles, a cruel reminder of what happened.

Emma got married. One morning, Joyce called her right after she got to school. She had forgotten an assignment and asked Emma to drop it off. She put a robe over her night gown, put on her slippers and left the house. She was not quite awake yet. She ran a stop sign and got hit by a truck. The driver got out and they exchanged insurance information. Emma could not get her car started and she had no intention of getting out of her vehicle, so this kind man, Bob, pulled her car with her in it to school, where he got out and gave Joyce her papers. Then he pulled her home and Emma thanked him profusely. Out of the blue he asked her if she was married and when Emma told him that she wasn't anymore, he asked her if she'd like to have dinner with him that evening and Emma surprised herself by saying that she would like that. Bob was a contractor in Houston and he was in Austin for four days, helping his mother move into a condominium. Emma met her later and she told me that she and Grandma would get along famously. Anyway. They saw each other two more times before he went back to Houston. Emma hoped that was not the end of the relationship, and it wasn't. He started spending week-ends with Emma. After about a month of that, he asked her to marry him. Emma put her arms around this sweet man and told him, "Yes, what took you so damned long?" Bob laughed and asked her if it would be at all possible for her to work on her language, at least until after the wedding, because he didn't want her to say, "Shit yes, of course I do" when the justice of the peace asked her if she would take this man, etc. Emma kissed him and told him, "Fuck yes, I'll do anything for you." There were about twenty people at their wedding and when the moment came, Emma looked at Bob and said, very slowly, "Yes. I. Do." It is nice to see Emma so happy and Bob is just wonderful. Bob and Emma got married just before Joyce graduated from high school and, after she was all settled in college, Emma sold her house and moved to Houston. We get together often, and next spring, Emma, Bob, Dad and I are going on a cruise together. Emma is making all the arrangements, which is a bit scary.

Dad is still into running and jogging, and last year he and Dean flew to the east coast and ran the Boston marathon, all 26 miles. Pam and I were as proud of them as they were of themselves. They want to do it again next year.

Dean did graduate in three years, but I am sure that does not surprise you. The girl of his dreams became the love of his life when he married Pam after graduating. Pam never liked her father and did not invite him to the wedding. She thought the world of Bob, who was so good to Emma and to her and her sisters, and asked him to walk her down the aisle. Bob was moved and thrilled and told Pam that this was an honor, but he did not want to hurt her dad's feelings. Emma quickly assured him that her ex didn't have any. When they got married, Pam had just finished summer school and had only one year of college to go. Like Dean, she also graduated in three years. I cried so much at their wedding, Sam, and they weren't all tears of happiness. I thought about how wonderful it would have been to see you there as Pam's maid-of-honor and I missed you so very much. Sidney was Dean's best man, and Sam, John was his grooms-man. Oh God, how you would have loved that wedding.

John is at the Air Force Academy in Colorado Springs, and he's doing very well. I write him occasionally and he calls us from time to time, and he stops by the house when he is in town, which is not very often. Pam and Dean drove out to see him sometime last year.

Hope is doing fine, Sam. She missed you terribly, and all she wanted to do besides eat was sleep on your bed, and she did that for months. Dad and I enrolled her in obedience classes about a year-and-a-half ago, but that did not go over very well. All the other dogs seemed way ahead of her, and Dad and I felt like parents pushing their mentally challenged four-year-old into attending kindergarten with regular students. When the trainer blew that damned whistle, Hope got scared, and she would lie down and cry and look up at us with those sad eyes. Dad and I couldn't stand it, and, after the second time, we decided we didn't care if she didn't know when or how to sit, roll, stop, etc. We loved her just the way she was and why did she have to know any of those commands anyway when she's never more than a few inches away from our heels, or she's in our arms or on our bed.

Sam, a few months ago, we cried for joy when Pam gave birth to a tiny, healthy and adorable little boy, whom they named Adam. Pam's water broke when she was taking her last final and someone called Dean, and he rushed over and took her to the hospital and little Adam was born just a few hours later. Pam and Dean are the sweetest parents and Dean is doing his share of diapering, just like Dad did when you and Dean were babies. Last week end, Grandma and Grandpa flew over to see their first great-grandchild. When Grandma held Adam in her arms for the first time, she looked up at me and said, "Well, Helen. I think that this sweet, innocent and beautiful little baby resembles you." I gave Grandma a hug and thanked her for her sweet words. Yes, Sam, I am really making an effort to get along better with her, and she is also trying very hard and it's all going to be all right.

Sweetheart, you're never far from my thoughts and you'll live in my heart forever.

Good night, Honey, I love you.

All my love.

Always, Mom

p.s. God, thank You very much. My cup runneth over again.

0-595-31763-4